INDRA DAS

This special signed edition is limited to **1000** numbered copies.

This is copy 791.

The Last Dragoners of Bowbazar

The Last Dragoners of Bowbazar

INDRA DAS

Subterranean Press 2023

The Last Dragoners of Bowbazar
Copyright © 2023 by Indrapramit Das.
All rights reserved.

Dust jacket illustration
Copyright © 2023 by Tran Nguyen.
All rights reserved.

Interior design
Copyright © 2023 by Desert Isle Design, LLC.
All rights reserved.

Edited by Navah Wolfe

First Edition

ISBN
978-1-64524-087-7

Subterranean Press
PO Box 190106
Burton, MI 48519

subterraneanpress.com

Manufactured in the United States of America

For my uncle and friend Aveek, who was the first to tell me to read Borges, the first to lend me a copy of Woolf's *Orlando*. If I could give this book to you in person, I would.

I do not care what comes after;
I have seen the dragons on the wind of morning.

— Ursula K. Le Guin,
The Farthest Shore

~1~

I HAVE A MEMORY of my grandmother showing me the strange flowers of a tree quite unlike anything I'd known to be real. We were standing in a garden—a cloak of chill mist thrown over it and embroidered in the gold of the dawn sun. The tree—or bush—was quite small, low to the ground, and looked like it was dying in an autumnal wilt, its thin, curling branches bare except for desiccated brown seed pods that hung heavy in the hazy air. My grandmother gestured for me to come closer, to see how the trunk and branches were covered in a fine fur. In her soiled hand, unwrinkled by the later toll of time, she took one of the dried brown seed pods—or flowers, or fruit—hanging above me and gently lowered it so I could see.

It wasn't a seed pod at all. With practiced care she nudged open the curled, broad leaves, unwrapping it to reveal what was inside.

The broad petals of the pod were the brown wings of a creature that fit gently in the pink cradle of my grandmother's palm like a bat. Its tail was the thin stem that connected it to the branches of the tree. And curled inside the embrace of its own wings was the contracted body of the beast, its six limbs clutched to its torso in insectile fragility, its sharp and thorny head like a flower's pistil, the curled neck covered in a dew-dusted mane of white fur like the delicate filaments of a dandelion seed. The gems of its eyes were left to my imagination, because they were closed in whatever deep sleep it was in.

"It's a dragon," I said, to encase the moment in the amber of reality.

"Yes, it is," said my grandmother with a proud smile. Whether this was pride at me or the little dragon whose papery brown wings she was touching, or both, I can't say. "Here, we call it the winged rose of Bengal."

It was the most beautiful thing I'd seen in my life. I remember the immensity of the happiness I felt, looking at this flower-like fetus of a dragon growing off a tree tended to by my grandmother, knowing that dragons were actually real and grew on trees, wondering if people knew.

I couldn't really believe it, which is why the memory became a dream. I convinced myself it wasn't a true memory, because dragons don't exist.

Why didn't I ask my grandmother later? My family? I did, of course, and they said: "Dragons aren't real, you had a dream." If the dragon tree was a real thing, and my family had the privilege of caring for such a marvel, why would they only show it to me once, when I was young, just old enough to know about dragons from books and cartoons and movies on pirated VHS tapes?

Dragons aren't real. I told myself I'd made them real in this dream because my father had written about them in his short career as an author (I was too young to read his novel *The Dragoner's Daughter* at the time, but he'd still read me a few passages), and because I had read his time-yellowed copy of Tolkien's *The Hobbit* many times and imagined Smaug in the sky-stretched shadows of monsoon clouds. The dragons I saw hanging from those trees were nothing like what I had imagined, though.

I know now that forgetting and remembering was a cycle I have relived many times, a snake eating its tail.

~2~

WHEN I WAS in school, I was called the snake from nowhere.

What my classmates at St. Lorenzo School for Boys meant was that I didn't know where I was from. I was Indian, of course—brown and black haired, like them, that went without saying, but it didn't count. When asked what my family *was*, I shrugged and said I didn't know. This was the truth. I didn't know whether we were Hindu or Muslim or Christian or God Only Knows. I didn't know whether we were Bengali or Anglo-Indian or Marwari (I know Bangla, English, and a little bit of Hindi, but so do a lot of people in West Bengal). I 'looked', according to my classmates, Chinese or North-Eastern, like a Naga, by which they meant a tribal from the corner-tucked state of Nagaland, also a word for 'snake'. I had a Christian surname (George) and an odd first name (Reuel) but didn't seem to know much about Christianity. So they called me the snake from nowhere. I told them that snakes don't have narrow eyes, which they gave me as the reason I looked North-Eastern. They ignored this logic, because logic is no friend of cruelty or racism. My skin was as brown as theirs, but I was forever different.

The snake from nowhere.

Realizing that we don't live in a country (or world) where someone can choose to be free of the weight of ethnicities and religions and other markers of identity, I was taken out of school in class 6 and home-schooled by my family. They had gotten me into St. Lorenzo on the basis of our family name, but they hadn't really trained me in the pretense of being Christian. They had underestimated how difficult it is to be no one for a child.

But when I asked my family who we were, where we were from, their vague answers essentially said 'nowhere' too. We were the only family in Calcutta without any ethnicity. Of course, this isn't possible. Everyone born on Earth has an ethnicity. It is, unfortunately, a signature left on our persons by god. That is to say, it is a signature left on us by our own hand, which has learned to write, and describe how we are different from each other, and how we may protect each other from our own hatreds by clinging to the packs and tribes we have made with language.

My family had an ethnicity. I just didn't know what it was. This will seem today like a sinister act of gaslighting on my family's part. And it was that, in a way. But I do realize now, as an adult, that where my family 'comes from', where our ancestors come from, is hard to describe. Because it's not, in the traditional sense of the word, a real place, or a real culture. At least, our language has made it unreal. Our rules have made it unreal. Our world has made it unreal.

As my parents sometimes said when I asked where our family was from: "You wouldn't believe it if we told you."

Better to be no one than branded crazy.

~3~

A MEMORY: MY grandmother digging into a hole in the soil of the garden courtyard with her bare hands, her fingernails darkening to black moons with dirt. Next to her was a checkered cloth bundle—something wrapped in a gamcha. My father crouched next to her with a spade, and had probably started the pit with it. When the hole in the damp ground (perhaps she waited for rains to soften it) was about four feet deep, she unwrapped the bundle next to her. I could smell the heavy aroma of damp earth wafting out of the trough.

The delicacy with which she unfolded the wrap reminded me of someone handling a newborn baby—swaddling or un-swaddling it. There was instead an egg under the cloth, huge and pale as the moon in the sky. I couldn't tell whether the shell was the colour of moonlight, or whether it was the moonlight that gave it its pearlescent glow. It hurt the eye to look at, with a fractal shimmer that gave it a spiraling depth, as if it held an infinite curling staircase within its spherical shape, an unhatched Fibonacci spiral hiding gelatinously within its shell.

My grandmother cradled the egg, which was about the size of a human infant, and gently placed it in the ground. Then, carefully, she buried it—again, with her bare hands, before my father took over. It was like a funeral, a burial, as solemn, but there was something joyous in the way my grandmother's mouth twitched back a smile. I was watching her against the warmth of my mother, who held me hoisted in her arms, her flesh humming with a song she was singing along with the rest of our family, who stood all around my grandmother and father as they knelt and completed the burial of the egg. There was no light in the courtyard except what was reflected of the cosmos by the night sky, and what was reflected of the city by the air below the very same. The moon was nearly full, and the stars visible. The light was clear, our shadows strong. The family sang, a song that sounded mournful, in a language that I couldn't understand, but it surged with a life that seemed to come from beyond the lights above this world.

~4~

I ONCE ASKED my mother, when I was still in school, "Maa, are we Naga?"

She paused in the middle of beating bedsheets with a broom. "Are your friends teasing you again?"

"No," I lied, not wanting to be interrogated about being bullied again.

She tsked and beat the bed harder than before, raising a cloud of motes that defined the light from the window, which framed her like a charcoal drawing, her numerous serpentine braids biting at the small of her back. I sneezed.

"The Nagas are their own people. We don't belong to their people, we have our own. People want to know where you're from so they can feel like they know something when they don't. People will see your eyes, and they will say you're a Naga or a Mizo or from China, because they think they know those people or those places, they think those places are foreign, even Nagaland, and that makes them better than you, because they're not foreign."

Maa was a solemn person, and hated to waste her breath on idle words. This was more than she ever talked in one go. To my surprise, she went on, both talking and beating the bed. "People. Don't. Know. Anything. About. Nagaland. Or China," she said, and stopped to wipe her forehead and let the broom rest against her hip. "They especially don't know anything about who we are and where we're from. Narrow minds can't hold true places. Will you remember that? People don't know anything."

I sneezed again.

"Do you have a cold?" asked Maa, unaffected by the dust thickening the light from the window.

"Where *are* we from, then?" I asked.

"I've told you."

"You never tell me."

"I do. We come from nomadic people. We move around. There are many of us around the world, but we're solitary, and don't like to draw attention."

"We don't have a religion?"

"What we worship is no business of anyone else's. The place we have come to, our family, as nomads, is here. Calcutta. If someone asks, the only answer that matters is that we are Indian. Understood? We live in this country like them."

"Do I have a passport?"

"No."

"Don't I need one to be Indian?"

"Don't be like these nosy ones in school. You don't need anything but the body you're using to be in a place to be here. Now go and do your homework."

"Do you and Baba have passports?"

"Go do your homework or you'll get a slap."

ANOTHER TIME, I asked my father why we had a Christian name if we're not Christian.

"It's just a name, Ru. Names don't belong to religions," he said, cleaning his glass pipe.

"Baba, the boys in school say they do."

"Oho, the boys in school don't know everything," he said, stroking his beard. An echo of Maa's refrain of *nobody knows anything*. "But. Since you've asked, we have the name George because St. George once slew a dragon. There's a nice irony to that," he said, sounding more than a little smug, as if a pre-teen boy couldn't possibly understand what he was on about. He was right—I had no idea what the irony was, but I held what he'd said my head, having seen pictures of St. George and the dragon in our house.

When the boys at school teased me during break time, I told them, "We are Indian but descended from St. George who killed a dragon." They told me boys who looked like me couldn't be descended from Christian saints. Which made little sense to me, since the Christian boys in school were no less brown than the boys who weren't. I landed a punch on Joseph, the short but prickly Anglo-Indian boy who'd led this response with his relished pronunciation of racial slurs. He fell like a tree, but his tooth notched a scar in one of my knuckles, a dragon's bite, justice coursing through my veins. I was suspended (and given a painful tetanus shot and a less painful but still-firm slap from my mother).

TO MY SURPRISE, when I returned to school after my two-day suspension, Joseph came to me during lunch break on the sun-baked school field and gave me a sullen apology.

He was wary, as if warding off another punch. His lip was scabbed by the history of our recent encounter. I felt more powerful than I had ever felt at school, hearing the words *I'm sorry I hit you.* I accepted with a wordless nod, benevolent but strong.

My attack had stirred the collective imagination. St. George lived in my blood. I'd seeded a story there, in the heads of the boys. That I was descended from dragon-killers. They didn't want to be friends with the snake from nowhere, but they respected him now. I was also St. George the killer of serpents. The snake eats its tail.

So I kept telling stories, as currency for respect. To make up for my nowhereness. When classmates came up to me and asked what it was like to punch Joseph, I'd grab the opportunity to tell them more about where my courage and ferocity came from. I told them about how my parents kept dragon shrines in our big old house, that we worshipped what we killed, and ate dragon flesh, and came from a secret place. We were nomads from the great unknown, come to Calcutta on the swift wings of beasts we had tamed. In the evenings we drank cups of blood instead of tea, in supplication to the curling bronze serpents on our walls, winged in incense.

Some of these things were true to me at the time. Some of these things were not true. Some of these things were truer than I knew. But whatever the truth, the Georges became known as a secret dragon cult among my classmates. This was my vindication.

One of those hot days on the shimmering field, my classmate Ranjan brought me a pale lizard that he claimed had fallen from the sky. He was short, wide-eyed and lost in his oversized uniform. He reminded me of Gollum from *The Hobbit* in his sordid excitement as he held the animal by its tail, making it dance with his twitching.

"I saw it fall out of the sky! Is it a dragon?"

"Yes," I said, feeling overwhelmed by some strange recognition as I looked at the pale gecko. It dropped from Ranjan's fingers to the sand-choked grass. The animal swiped the air with its limbs, barely alive. It had probably fallen from the beak of a kite or a crow, if it had indeed fallen out of the sky.

"Where are the wings?" Ranjan asked.

"Don't be an idiot, that's a tiktiki," said another student who had come up to look.

"You can't tell, it's all bloody. Lizards don't fly. But where are the wings?" said Ranjan.

"Snake boy is lying and you're a fool," said the newcomer. I glared at him, clenching my bandaged fist to remind him of my propensity for battle. He said nothing.

"The wings are delicate when they're this small. Like spiderwebs. It wasn't ready to fly. They probably tore away in the wind," I said.

The newcomer snorted and walked away to rejoin the informal football match on the other side of the field. Ranjan was enthralled. "Kill it, St. George," he whispered.

I picked up a stone and flattened the false dragon into the dust. I told myself it was mercy, but made my face contort in anger, an ancient warrior fulfilling his birthright. Ranjan put his hands to his head and sprang away gibbering like a goblin. I left the bloody stone and walked away, not daring to pick it up and look underneath it, hoping this would look cold and composed to my spectator. A shadow slithered across my sunlit head and swept over the ground of the field at that moment. Something winged, perhaps the kite that had grabbed the gecko. I walked away from my small murder, sweating.

~5~

A MEMORY: MY parents in the garage behind our house, with the folding metal door shut and a naked bulb glossing the wet concrete ground. The inside of the garage was far larger than it should be, from what it looked like from the outside. There were sleek black dragons—or drakes, which were immature dragons, they said—in the huge aquariums lined against the wall. They were whiplashed with swirling hairs or filaments, and hard to look at for their gleaming darkness. The aquariums weren't lit by electric lights, but the water had a blue-green luminescence of its own. This I recognized as the excretions of the drakes as they thrashed in the water—which Baba, forever myth-obsessed, called halahala after the poison produced into the Ocean of Milk when the devas and asuras churned it to find the nectar of immortality, using a mountain as a churning rod and the nagaraja Vasuki, king of serpents, as the churning rope. In that moment I knew that the halahala-infused water was one of the ingredients of the Tea of Forgetfulness.

Maa thrust her arms in the sloshing water. Grappling with the oil-slick drake, she tossed it to the floor while Baba chanted the words of our ancestors. I sprang back as the drake sleeked across the wet stone, hard to pin down with a gaze, its chitinous black form looking like a giant crustacean at times, a serpent at others. Maa took a swig from a glass bottle with a brown liquid inside. Baba had lit a flame on a metal wand that he handed to her with practiced ease, runners passing a baton. With a flourish, she grabbed the torch, bent over the churning black storm of jet scales and spikes and sinew slapping and sliding across the floor, and spat into the torch. A tongue of flame emerged from her mouth as the kerosene ignited, washing over the drake for a second that lit up the dim garage. I basked in the heat of it. Maa waved the torch in her hand, took another mouthful of kerosene, and licked the drake with her glowing tongue of fire again, the water on its back and folded wings sizzling and steaming so the room grew hazy.

Under the blankets of steam swaddling it, the drake had slowed its movement, relaxing into a sinuous throb. Maa was barking sounds at it, while Baba ran his hand over its back in quick strokes, his face tight against the heat.

My grandmother, who was holding me to her soft, large belly, told me in our language, "A dragon Queen will lick its young to soothe them. Your Maa is giving it memories of that, before it gives its body to us to eat."

"Why do we have to eat it?"

"The serpent must eat its tail. We are the serpent," my grandmother whispered.

"Was it drowning in the water?"

"Sweet child," she stroked my hair. "It's not in pain. It's amphibious. The water tells this one its story, tells it not to grow the flame in its belly and burn down our house. It can live in ocean and sky. Here, it's caught between both. Its churning is a memory of how its ancestors swam across stars and sea, and in its churning it gives us forgetfulness, so you might live in the now of the world while keeping the name of its kin alive."

~6~

THE DAY I slew the false dragon on the school field, Ranjan and his friend Neil jumped off the school bus with me, and asked me to show them my house, sanctum of the secret dragon cult. I wasn't allowed to bring friends home, but I didn't know what else to do. My family lived in a big house in Bowbazar. A traditional old Calcutta house, built by our ancestral settlers in the 1930s, with thick walls, three stories, palatial verandahs that wound around the structure like serpents through which I'd run like a swallowed mouse as a child.

I took my two classmates home, five minutes from the school bus stop. We passed the Crystal Dragon Chinese Restaurant Cum Bar at the front of the house (leased out, though it helped people in the neighborhood assume we were Chinese), down the small alley by the side of the building, drying clothes flapping from the windows above us, to a door in the side. They gaped at the yellow hand-painted sign with red letters above the door, which read: BOWBAZAR DRAGONERS CLUB (est. 1942). Few in Calcutta know about this club, except as an urban legend about a restaurant that serves dragon meat. There are reasons for this.

"What's a drag-on-er?" asked Ranjan, excited.

"Like a falconer," said Neil knowingly. Unlike Ranjan, Neil was smooth and round, his amiable head fuzzed with close-cropped hair and decorated with heavy spectacles. I felt nervous. We entered the doorway and went up the steep stairwell to the first floor.

The Dragoners Club wasn't like the Saturday Club or the Calcutta Club or the other clubs the bhadraloks of the city inherited from the British, with their big old campuses of mansions and greens and restaurants (I'd never been inside those, only seen their walls in passing). This was more like the Chinese social clubs of the two Chinatowns, little more than some big rooms where our community gathered to play cards and carom, and an adjoining canteen where people ate. I'd pass the club rooms every day on the way back from school. It was usually filled with extended family—my parents, my aunts and uncles, who I don't remember well, which I'll get to later. Then there were the other permanent members, our 'people', who lived elsewhere in the city and weren't strictly family, but treated as such because they shared the same secrets we did, and looked like us, and came, like us, I assumed, from nowhere. The club room and canteen had plain yellow walls covered in artwork, and dim overhead bulbs in shades reflecting off the blood-red Formica of the tables. The windows on one side looked on to the verandah and the courtyard, on the other side, to the birdshit-speckled walls of the adjacent building. That side was often covered by heavy curtains.

That day, everyone turned to stare at the newcomers as we entered the Dragoners Club. My schoolmates coughed in the thick cigarette smoke which hung like dragon's breath over our heads. My mother came to greet us, and didn't look pleased. Greeted by her formidable stare, Neil and Ranjan quickly turned shy. But she was polite, and offered the boys lunch at the club canteen. Baba was delighted, breaking from his card game with his cousins to boast about our food. "Boys, boys! This is where you come to eat a whole dragon! You picked just the right day to come visit us, we're having the full platter. It's not easy to prepare, I'll tell you that much," he laughed, peering down at us from behind his round wire-frame glasses. I felt a surge of pride at the wonder in the boys' eyes, at the dragon sculptures, the artwork all over the walls, and Baba's long, Gandalf-like beard. There were paintings, woodcuts, drawings and prints of dragons from all the continents—from Níðhöggr to Vritra, Apep to the Dragon Kings of the Four Seas.

"You have to become temporary members to eat at the Dragoners Club, boys," said Baba. This was the rule. They signed the ledger, and my father paid their ten rupee fees. The signature declared, as with any walk-ins to the canteen, that the Temporary Member would never tell anyone the location of the club (even though there was a sign, albeit on the side of the house), and would forever forget the experience afterwards. Ranjan and Neil were thrilled at these clandestine flourishes.

I usually ate upstairs in our normal dining room, not at the club canteen. But on that day, I ate the 'whole dragon' platter with Ranjan and Neil, with my family, and my aunts and uncles, all watching. "It's actually a drake, a very young dragon, asked to immolate itself in its own flame, in a chamber of water, as an honourable sacrifice to a world of restricted possibilities," Baba explained, while my Maa smoked a bidi in the corner. The food was already laid out. The signature entrée was placed in the centre of one of the tables, so huge it was spilling off the steel tray. The thing on the dish looked to me like a giant, serpentine crustacean curled into itself in a spiral, its head, limbs and legs docked as too large for the platter, though it was jagged with spines and long hairs like antennae. Smoke wisped off its plated scales, as if it was fresh out of the fire. There was a smell of charcoal that cut through the cigarette smoke. The boys ate the starter rice in a stupor of disbelief, as Baba helped pry open the charred black carcass with what looked like ornate pliers to get at the flesh. "Don't let him trick you. It's a big fish," Maa called out from the corner, noticing Neil's scared look. It was a half-hearted attempt at best. My head reeled from the pungent steam that gushed out from under the black scales of the drake. "I bet you're wondering where the wings are," Baba muttered, licking the corner of his mouth as he opened the carcass. "These drakes don't fly. Many types of dragons, like in stories. Think of this like a chicken, instead of a big eagle."

My grandmother, who had sat placidly and smiled at us until then, clicked with her tongue, reached out to touch the carcass and then her forehead. "Don't disrespect."

Baba gave her a puckish smile. "Ai-oh, just making the children feel at home." There was a loud snap as he wrenched another scale back. They looked like black metal under the bulbs. Maa stubbed out her bidi in an ashtray on the next table and came over, impatient. With a curved knife she helped Baba cut the meat, which was glowing faintly as if it were a soft mirror reflecting the bulb above it.

The flesh Baba and Maa peeled and sliced out from under the scales of the drake was cloud-white and wet, veined with thread-fine capillaries of lightning. Like flesh carved from the belly of a sky fat with rain. There was nothing to go with the dragonflesh—just plain rice with a drizzle of soy sauce (the soy sauce was absolutely *not* to go on the dragonflesh, Baba told us). My family and the club members at the other tables used their hands, sucking up the slices of lambent flesh with loud slurps, despite the chopsticks and cutlery on the table. My classmates and I used forks. The dragon flesh felt gelatinous and melted on the tongue, barely there, leaving a strong fishy, sea-salt aftertaste laced with the heady aroma of petrol. "Would fish disappear on your tongue like a breeze before a storm?" Baba asked us. Maa rolled her eyes. I had tasted this before, I knew, but barely remembered.

"That's it?" asked Ranjan, sticking out his tongue. "It's like...smelly air."

Baba smiled. "It's insubstantial because asking a drake to cook itself like this makes it exist in a way it was not meant to. It is both here and not, not of this world. It has become a base shell of itself, preserving a memory. It takes practice to taste a memory, but when you do...ah! Then it will be real. You become one with beauty like no other."

Ranjan murmured, "St. George," looking at my father in admiration.

As we took more bites, there was a gathering heat in our mouths and throats. I could see the sweat shining on Ranjan and Neil's foreheads as they struggled to finish. I panted, but it did nothing. The heat of the flesh didn't taste like spice, didn't linger on the tongue and teeth so much as live in your cells like a slow electrocution. It felt like being nervous, excited, overwhelmed.

"Even a baby dragon too much for you, hm?" asked Baba. The aunts and uncles laughed, boisterous but good-natured. The boys looked stunned. My entire body was prickling, the hair on my arms and neck standing up. To my great embarrassment, I felt like crying. Thankfully, there were tears and sniffles all around, Neil and Ranjan's eyes wet as well, though no one was weeping like I suddenly wanted to, with the gift of this storm inside me, given to me by this dead, splayed dragon on the table. I could not believe that this was ordinary for my family, that I somehow could not know it.

"You will dream for weeks of worlds unseen, of serpents in sky and sea," Baba grinned, stroking his beard.

Neil and Ranjan couldn't finish their dragonflesh, stuffing their mouths with rice to stifle the burning and crackling inside them. I fancied I could see their teeth sparking through my swimming tears. I finished every last morsel on my plate. I was surprised to see Maa smiling at me before she got up to clear the plates. She got us foaming glasses of iced 7-Up and milk, which she said would help cool us down. Ranjan and Neil gulped theirs down, while I drank mine slow, letting the storm in me die out naturally, closing my eyes and feeling the flickers of light in the clouds of my eyelids, the rumbles of thunder in my stomach, the cool rain of sweat dripping down my temples, my father's affectionate hand briefly on the scruff of my neck. The aunts and uncles were talking softly to themselves in our language, the language of our people, and it felt as soothing as tossed pebbles dancing over a stream at that moment.

After the meal, we were served the Tea of Forgetfulness in little china bowls. It was given to all temporary members who found our 'restaurant' behind the more conventional restaurant upfront. The tea too smelled fishy, and was a dark, algae-green. The boys drank it with grimaces, the bitterness leaving stains on their tongues.

The tea wasn't just a symbolic novelty.

By the time Maa walked them to Chandni Chowk metro crossing ten minutes away to call them each a taxi home, they only had a vague idea of having skipped their bus stop for a gambol in Bowbazar. I never got to ask them what dreams the dragonflesh gave them, because I couldn't remember to ask.

I HAVE DRUNK the Tea of Forgetfulness all through my life, from when I was a child. My parents made it a daily ritual after meals, and before bedtime.

~7~

NOT LONG AFTER I brought my unexpected guests home, Maa took me to one of the many rooms in our house with the shrines that that I'd told my classmates about. They were collections—like downstairs, of art and sculptures of dragons from across cultures. The second-storey room she took me to had a scroll hanging on the plain whitewashed wall, bathed in the dusky light from a window, sunlight diffused by the narrow gaps between houses in the neighborhood. The scroll was a waxy yellow, and scrawled in a flowing script—the fire tongue my family spoke only at home. The language of our nonexistent people. I couldn't read it, but it flowed from my tongue with the atavistic ease of water flowing down a mountain. The script on the scroll was delicate, each character weaving into the other with lines like a dense spiderweb of ink, which formed the shape of a sinuous winged serpent. The inkwork was so fine the winged shape vanished into writing unless you were looking for it.

Maa sat me down on the floor by the scroll. She had her usual stoic expression on, but there was a flicker of concern in the set of her mouth. She placed her hands on my shoulders, and spoke in the fire tongue.

"Listen. I know Baba told you that we take the surname George because of St. George. And you told those boys that."

"Yes?"

She tsked, as she often did, her brow furrowing. "Baba shouldn't have done that. He was trying to be smart. He does that sometimes."

"So we're not named after St. George?"

Maa sighed deep in her chest, and looked down at the stone floor between us.

"We are, in a way, but it's a joke. It doesn't mean anything. Our names here don't mean anything. Our family chose 'George' because people don't look too hard at people who look like us but are Christians, in this city. We aren't Christian, you understand that, don't you?"

"Yes! But what about St. George?"

"Uff, never mind him. We're not descended from him. That's not what your father was saying, but he shouldn't have confused you like that. It was wrong of him, and disrespectful to our people."

"The nomads."

She smiled. "Yes. We don't vanquish dragons, like St. George. We respect them. If we kill them, it is for a reason, not because they represent evil or anything like that."

"So our people did kill dragons, then, once upon a time?" I said, my heart palpitating. Maa stared fixedly at me, as if wondering what to say.

"You're old enough to know that stories are a part of any people. They mean things without having to be entirely true. Like the Bible, yes? Jesus walking across water, and coming back to life. St. George killing that dragon. Or Hanuman leaping over the sea to Lanka in the Ramayana."

I nodded. Maa shook her head. She seemed in pain.

"Ah. The stories you're telling the boys at school...are more dangerous than you know. But," she looked me in the eyes. "That there is some truth in them, that you recognize despite everything, tells me that...we've put you in a difficult position and," I was scared to see that there were now tears in my mother's dark black eyes, just barely, but enough for the light in the room to twinkle off them like candle flames.

"It isn't fair to you. I know that. You were born under the wings of a serpent impossible. You deserve better than to be a boy from nowhere, in a crowded, suffering world where the sky is always above us, and never under us."

Then, she pinched the air in front of her face and moved her hand to the side. It was like an invisible veil parted reality, and her face was suddenly covered in tattoos that curled in snakes of intricate language along her cheekbones before slithering into the undergrowth of her hair and down the trunk of her neck. With both hands, Maa pulled the air again, and in her fingers, like a magic trick, hung a silky, thin scarf that she plucked out of invisibility from around her head. I looked at this new person, my mother born anew, looking like some strange warrior with tattoos all over her face.

She held out the sheets of translucent material, so thin they nearly disappeared from certain angles. I realized they were covered, like Maa's skin, in ink, though even finer—a mesh of script that ran up and down the scarf. The thought popped into my head, of how much money she could make selling such an astonishing article of clothing.

"This is my headscarf. I wear one all the time. So does your grandmother. It's…silk, pulled from the jaws of a serpent, with their permission. The writing on it makes my tattoos invisible. You can rewrite what people see, on it. It's made from a similar material as that," she said, looking up at the scroll hanging on the wall. "That is from the membranes of a wing."

"Is it magic?" I said, staring warily at Maa's inked face.

"I suppose yes," she smiled ever so briefly. "Like in all those books you and your father read. Touch," she said. I did, and it felt like touching a breeze, before it felt like simply touching my mother's hand, which I could see through the scarf.

"Do you know why I wear it?"

"Why?"

"Because these tattoos—the language on my face, they tell the story of another world, not this one. No one would understand what they say, or believe it. I wear this headscarf to keep those secrets safe. I have never seen that other world, but we come from it, and carry its memory."

"What does it say? The secrets?"

My mother's coarse palm against my forehead was a shock, because she rarely showed physical affection once I grew past the toddling years. She brushed my hair back. "Some of what it says must remain a secret. Some of it says that I am a rider, and a part of what I ride," she looked again at the scroll on the wall, and its serpent of language, scaled in the same script as her tattoos, the writing on the headscarf. "That is what we worship, if anything. It is why we eat their flesh and blood, and offer ours in death and life. To stay alive, for each other. We are a hive mind, and the serpent a legion of body. In this city, and this world, this space and time, this isn't something one can be easily. This world has become too small for that." I thought of cowboys and the Indians in another land across the oceans who weren't from India, of the riders of Rohan and the dragonlords of Earthsea. But mostly, I thought about Baba's novel, the glimpses he'd read to me.

"I don't understand," I said, though something inside of me did.

She nodded, and lifted the scarf to her face. It was gone in an instant, and Maa's face was unadorned by ink, her hands moving around her head in a pantomime of wearing a headscarf. When she was done, she brushed her knuckles across her eyes. "I'm sorry, babushona," she said, allowing Bangla to slip in as she sometimes did. "We have to take you out of school. This kind of attention isn't good for us. People won't understand the kind of family we are. From now on, we'll teach you here at home."

I just nodded again, dazed, but more concerned by the sorrow on Maa's face than the prospect of leaving school. Because the truth was, I had no real friends there. I supposed I'd miss telling the boys the stories of our dragon-obsessed family, and gaining their respect.

Maa picked up a cup on the low wooden table under the scroll of the winged serpent. Steam curled out of it. "Please," she said. I recognized the mossy smell of the Tea of Forgetfulness. I drank it in reverent silence.

"Why won't you let me remember?" I dared ask.

She blinked. "You deserve to be real in this world. It's not an easy thing to be stuck between worlds."

But stuck I was, and ever have been.

I SOMETIMES STOOD in the courtyard during dusk and looked up at the labyrinth of the house wrapping around it, the fading square of light that was the sky above, brush-stroked with the leaves and branches of the great tree rustling above me, streaked with the darting silhouettes of dozens of bats. I remember looking closely, and seeing that some of the flitting creatures weren't bats at all, that they trailed the bristled threads of tails, that there was a sharpness to their heads and elongated necks, but it was hard to focus. They were too fast, and mimicked the wheeling of the bats too well.

Above them, the stars would come out.

~1~

I WAS TWO YEARS away from teenage when I stopped being a schoolboy. My private tutors were dull, weighed down by heat and exhaustion. I became more restless, ever drawn to the house library, my personal Alexandria. I buried myself deeper in Baba's collection of foreign science fiction, fantasy, and horror books, most brought by an old and estranged friend from the United States. I went through stacks of mythic retellings in the Amar Chitra Katha comics my parents had bought me over the years, pored over hardcover coffee-table tomes on history, mythology, and astronomy. My entire sex education was patched together from fiction and illustrated texts on reproductive biology and sex my parents left lying around (including an illustrated English edition of the *Kama Sutra*, bless them), perhaps in the hope I'd absorb their knowledge without them having to intervene.

I began asking why I didn't have any siblings, or cousins, why none of the people who showed up to eat and play cards at the Dragoners Club had any children. "They do, they just don't bring them," my parents would say, pretending to be busy. These questions clearly made my parents uncomfortable. When I asked my grandmother in her room, she would pat the bed she lay on for her afternoon siestas. "Isn't your Didima enough company?" she'd ask, and I would bury my face in her talcum-scented belly. Her robes would glisten in the shade of her room, turning iridescent or changing colour entirely from their usual white, depending on the tilt of sunlight from behind the curtains of the doorway.

~2~

THE DAY I turned thirteen, my parents gave me my first real birthday 'party'. They arranged a special dinner at the Crystal Dragon. It was special not because of the venue, which was after all right downstairs from home, but because they'd invited a guest my age—Alice, who was the daughter of the Crystal Dragon's proprietors. My parents, even in their infinite distraction, had begun to worry about my lack of peers. The Chens had always been nice to me. When I was in school, I'd go downstairs in the early evenings, when the Crystal Dragon was relatively empty. I did my homework there in the dim cool of the windowless restaurant, surrounded by the sour tang of vinegar and hot sauce. Uncle or Auntie Chen (one of whom was usually in the kitchen, their office, or behind the counter) would give me free bottles of cold Thums-Up or appetizers like their outrageously salty chicken Drums of Heaven with daintily foil-wrapped bones. The Chens lived in a flat not too far away, in Tiretta Bazar. I only saw Alice in the restaurant some weekends, when she'd come over to help her parents or just lounge around there. Perhaps I never really noticed that I was always waiting for her silhouette to darken the rectangle of daylight hovering at the end of the long, narrow restaurant. For the brief wave we'd share before I went back to my homework, unable to do it for a few minutes after. We'd seen each other grow up in these glimpses within the cool belly of the Crystal Dragon.

Despite their livelihood being innately tied to our home, the Georges had always interacted at a polite remove with the Chens. It prevented complications. So my thirteenth birthday dinner at the Chens' restaurant was unusual, a hesitant merging of our agreed upon boundaries (the Chens definitely knew we weren't part of the Chinese Indian communities of the city).

Alice's parents didn't join us for dinner, because they were busy with the restaurant, but did show up often to ask us how the food was (it was good, and outrageously salty as expected). Alice, in a striped red-and-white collared polo shirt (which might as well have been a bedazzling dress to me), jeans, and sneakers, her hair neatly middle-parted, said an awkwardly cheerful 'happy birthday' and laid a matte red envelope by my cutlery and plate before sitting down with us. Giving me a card in addition to showing up for dinner felt like a startling kindness to me. I barely managed to stutter out my thanks (in the envelope, which I'd open later in my room as if it were a top secret communiqué, was a crisp one hundred rupee note, a birthday card with a photo of puppies wishing me a happy birthday, and her own neat handwriting doing the same inside in ballpoint, signed with her name and a smiley face). She looked uncomfortable, which I couldn't blame her for.

My parents did most of the talking through dinner, as we went through hot and sour soup, golden fried prawns, chilli roast pork, crispy Hakka noodles, burnt garlic fried rice. I found out more than ever before about Alice, who years ago had stared at me with fierce and unsated curiosity while peeping on tiptoes behind the counter of the Crystal Dragon, whose hair clips now flashed like the ends of an unseen diadem. I learned that she went to an international school, where they didn't need to wear uniforms. She liked to sing, and wanted to get as good at it as Celine Dion and Whitney Houston. She wanted to learn guitar like her brother. She liked watching movies and reading, even the classics from the school syllabus. When we checked the Chinese zodiac printed on our laminated placemats, I found that we were both born in the Year of the Rat (not the Dragon, whose tiny red ink apparition I touched lightly to acknowledge its familiar presence), almost the same age (she was a few months older).

The safe distance between us all those years made me afraid to look at Alice directly. It felt impossible to be sitting and having a normal conversation with someone who looked like me but wasn't family, who might have heard the same slurs thrown at her. Her hair was straighter than my wavy locks (down to my shoulders now, grown out like the rest of my family after I left school), but she still looked more like me than any of my classmates had. I wasn't a snake from nowhere to Alice—just the silent kid next door to her parents' workplace. That she was a girl made it all the more rare and strange, since I'd only ever known women as family or teachers. The feeling that came over me, sitting next to her, was familiar in a way I couldn't place—some shadow of a dream where I had eaten flesh marbled with lightning, and felt it crackle through me and make my heart lighter.

When my parents got up to talk to the Chens at the counter, Alice, with a look of panic at this unparented silence, asked me, "Is your hair always that long?"

"Yeah," I said, and laughed as if she'd made a joke.

"That's cool. None of the boys in my class have long hair," she said.

I didn't know what to say to that. It felt thrilling to be othered in a way that didn't make me feel lesser. I searched her face in furtive glances for some hidden malice.

"Yeah, it's part of our, um, culture," I ventured.

"I didn't know that. Like samurais and stuff, right?"

"Oh we're not Japanese," I said, though I wanted to cry out to her, *yes, just like samurais, I am a warrior but descended from St. George.* I had never felt prouder.

"Oh, I know," she laughed nervously. "I just meant like."

"It's okay. We, we don't, my family doesn't really talk about where we're from, so it's hard to tell. For other people," I stammered.

Luckily, my parents returned and quickly hogged the attention again.

That night, my envy for my parents' ability to talk to Alice with such ease was vast as the sky. But despite my creeping embarrassment at not instantly transforming into a dashing conversationalist, I wouldn't have traded places with anyone in the world right then as I turned a teenager, no longer just a boy, at least to myself. And, perhaps, to Alice. I felt like Baba and Maa had given me the best birthday present possible. After dinner, Uncle and Auntie Chen brought out the black forest cake my parents had gotten from Flury's. The candy-striped candles licked the dim air of the Crystal Dragon as everyone sang (*Happy birthday Roo-ELL*), even some of the strangers at other tables. The hum of reality coursed through me. I felt noticed. We were still in our house, our home, our cocoon, *my* cocoon, but I had emerged, partially. My breath, sweet with cola and spicy with hot sauce, vanquished the flames. Alice clapped, polite as ever.

I did learn how to talk to her, eventually.

~3~

ALICE CHEN AND I were slow to become friends.

A year of hesitant conversations at the Crystal Dragon passed before we started spending time together, as we both grew in tandem, our bodies changing, pimples and body hair blooming in concert with embarrassment. Even as this made us even more wary of each other, it made us more curious of each other as well, eager to see who the newly forming human opposite was.

For so many years, I'd felt like a child from nowhere, who belonged nowhere but inside the walls of my family's house. With Alice, I was somewhere. I was outside, in Calcutta, finally, overcoming my fear of venturing beyond (everywhere I'd gone, I'd gone inside taxis with my parents). She was the one who took me on my first metro ride, despite Chandni Chowk station being ten minutes from my house all my life. "Could you *be* any more innocent," she said to me, nearly singing. I followed her faithfully into the underground, eyes on her bouncing ponytail and bright pink backpack, the straps contrasting with her baggy black Metallica tee. She strode past the subway gates with self-aware confidence, and giggled maniacally when I slammed into the steel bars while fumbling my ticket, her cheeks pink, giddy on her own worldliness. I was mortified yet content to embrace my role as the helpless home-schooled kid, if it meant having a friend. I liked the pride in her eyes.

The squeak of her sneakers against the newly mopped marble floors of the platform was music to me, this fluorescent underworld we adventured through, she the wise guide, as exciting to me as vast Moria, given light and life by her grace, people all around, the darkness in the tunnel swelling with light, the rumble of the approaching Balrog only she could tame, and so she did, feet away from its screeching and hissing, its flashing skin, my guide and savior Alice stood nonchalant, her hair drifting in its fell breath. We rode the train in the late afternoon crowd, crushed together, hair gusting and intermingling in the stale tunnel air from the partly open windows. Our bodies so close and swaying as if in monotonous dance, the thunder in our feet and bones so reminiscent of something lost, our sweaty hands clutching a metal pole one under the other, bearing together the spear of St. George fixed through the heart of a roaring beast that ran beneath the city. It was no longer the Balrog roaming the tunnels of Moria. I saw the beast anew for what it was: a great silver serpent streaking through the earth, and we its riders. I felt a peculiar longing ache inside me, even though Alice was right there next to me, closer to me than ever before. I wondered what she was feeling. Her face, shining with sweat, was scrunched up in concentration as she peered at the diagram of the metro line and listened for the announcements so we wouldn't miss our stop (a brief ride southwards to Park Street, where we'd visit Oxford Bookstore and sit inside Kwality to eat ice cream sundaes on a fancy white tablecloth). She looked like the child she was, not a warrior-woman taming beasts alongside me, me the distinctly un-warrior-man. I wanted to hug her. I would, for the first time, at the end of that evening, her backpack heavier with the omnibus of *The Lord of the Rings* that I'd bought her.

~4~

"Dude, is this your grandma? She's so beautiful," said Alice. We were in my parents' library. She was looking at a framed black and white portrait on the wall. Alice was now allowed in the house (much to my surprise), though when I brought her upstairs most of the doors in the house were locked, guiding us only to certain rooms. The person in the photograph Alice was looking at was, indeed, beautiful, long locks flowing down their shoulders and beyond the frame, high cheekbones gathering shadows against the smooth slopes of their face, eyebrows dark as wounds above eyes that seemed to defy the monochrome and spark with impossible reflections. A large hooked ornament hung from one ear—possibly a fang or claw.

"That's actually my grandfather," I said.

"Whoa," Alice said, mouth open. "No way. He totally looks like a girl."

"My father told me I would keep asking if this was a picture of Didima, my grandmother upstairs. So, yeah. But it's Maa's father."

"Wow. He...does look a lot like Auntie."

"He died when I was young. I don't remember him too well. I think even in person, I used to think he was my other grandma, though Baba's mother died before I was born."

"Aw. Look at this, I love this...hat?"

"That's Didima," I said, as Alice looked at the portrait next to my grandfather's. Her face was squatter than my grandfather's long, elfin features, her voluptuous cheeks shining. Age had swaddled those plump, fierce features in soft wrinkles that she pampered with powder, no less dignified for it. She didn't look happy to be photographed, but carried herself proudly. She wore a large headdress—a crown of dark, jagged metal, from which emerged leathern folded wings that cowled her head and reached down to her shoulders.

"Maa and Baba told me that when my grandfather was young, there wasn't much difference between men and women in our culture. They would just be the same, and sometimes, men were pretty, and women were handsome or had beards. Or the other way around. And it didn't matter."

Alice looked at the photos, and then at me. I became conscious of my own long hair, and tried not to blush. She quickly looked away.

"That's really cool. I wish all cultures were like that," said Alice. "I love that everyone in your family has long hair like hippies." She strolled along the shelves of books and records.

"My mother's definitely no hippie. My father, on the other hand. My grandma, no way."

Alice had moved on down the shelves, and was examining the record cover for The Court of the Crimson King. The bubble she was blowing popped, and she licked the membrane of gum off her lower lip. "Okay. Don't be offended," she returned the album to the shelf. "I think, with the hair, you look a bit like a girl too. Like your grandpa," she said.

"Okay."

"Are you offended?"

"No. There's, nothing wrong with being a girl. So," I said, perhaps a little defensively.

Alice sat on the sofa next to my father's record player and stereo. "Sit, come here," Alice said, looking at me. I sat next to her. She was still looking at me. "I don't think there's anything wrong with being a girl either," she said, with a hint of a smile. She was fiddling with the green scrunchie around her right wrist. She took it off and patted my shoulder. "Turn around," she said. I did. Though her fingers didn't touch skin, I could feel the movements of her hands through my hair in the stirring of my roots. She gathered it all, letting air, warm with her imagined breath, caress the back of my neck, and with a playful yank she tied it into a ponytail using the scrunchie. I felt her pat my shoulder again, and turned around, dazed.

She smiled. "You can keep the scrunchie."

"Thanks. Thank you."

"You're welcome welcome. You always wear your hair down. Good to have a new look."

"Thanks. Maa braids my hair at home, but I don't wear it like that outside."

"You should." Alice squinted at me. "I think it's nice you didn't get angry when I said you look like a girl. Most boys would. I was hoping you wouldn't. And I was right. You didn't. Cus you're cool."

"If you called me an ugly girl, maybe I'd be a bit angry," I said, the words hurried and clumsy in my mouth. I realized now that she was checking to see if I was, indeed, angry. I wasn't—not now that I knew *she* didn't think a boy looking like a girl was a bad thing. I saw her relief when I smiled.

"No, you'd totally be a pretty girl," she said. "Half the guys in my class would get crushes on you."

"Okay, calm down," I said, my newly exposed neck radiating warmth.

Alice laughed. The sound of her chewing was conspicuous in the silence that followed. She rummaged in her pocket and brought out the gum wrapper to spit out her gum, packaged it into a tiny ball of paper, and put it back into the pocket of her shorts a little sheepishly. Feeling confused, I desperately tried to think of a joke.

"The thing about there being no difference between men and women back in the old days. In your family. Is that really true?" asked Alice.

"I guess. I mean, look at that portrait," I said, glad not have to tell a joke. "I don't really know. It was our old culture."

Alice looked pensive. "Boys are just...really. Really annoying, sometimes. Like even when I like a boy in class, I mean, want to be friends with a boy, they're always just joking and making fun of me."

"That sucks," I said, remembering the names I was called in school. "For being...you know, Chinese?"

"Did you get made fun of? When you were in school?" she asked.

"Yeah."

"I'm sorry," she said. "It's not that bad for me. The international students get more of that, the Asian ones. Mostly behind their backs. I mean I get teased about being Chinese too, but I call them lazy Bongs or whatever and they stop."

I smiled, thinking that Alice's mother was Bengali, which made Alice at least part-Bong too.

"This Japanese girl in our class, Yuiko—oh my god she was so cute—they say kawaii for cute—she taught me to say baka, it means fool. Like boka in Bangla. Poor Yuiko, they made fun of her accent a lot. I miss her, she went back to Japan. When the boys tease me, I call them boka bakas in Yuiko's honour. I can handle the teasing, but they're just, never serious with girls," she sighed. "They call me a boy because I like Metallica and stuff, but I like Britney too, and then they make fun of me for that, but they're just gross and all have the hots for her and want an excuse to keep talking about her. I bet they've seen her music video a thousand times. Then they keep making fun of each other for liking girls, like 'this dude has a crush on you' hardy har so funny. But no one actually says they like you."

"Do you want one of them to say that to you?"

She groaned and leaned back into the sofa, which creaked. "Maybe? Sometimes. Might be nice. Even if they are all boka. I just wish they'd grow up." Her forehead was shining—she was embarrassed at what she'd just admitted. I wondered, not for the first time, what it would be like to be Alice's classmate, to be one of these fabled boys. I'd never met them, though I'd met her girl friends a few times, and gone to see a couple of movies with the group at the New Market cinema halls.

"Anyway," Alice continued. "What I'm saying is that... you're not scared of girls. You're kind of shy, but I can talk to you properly. It's like you're old, in a way," she stopped, and added hurriedly, "Not like grandpa old. Mature. Maybe it's because of your culture. Your super mysterious culture." The multiple clocks on the walls ticked in unison, marking any silences in our conversation. Alice looked around, at the stacks of records, the shelves of video cassettes and books gathering dust and overflowing on to the carven wooden chairs and floor in haphazard towers, the old Bollywood posters on the walls side by side with prints of historical art from various cultures, the porcelain, resin, and wooden statues of dragons decorating the tables. Most of the rooms of our house always looked a bit like cluttered museum exhibits.

"Your family is so weird, Ru. In a good way. I've never met anyone who keeps *everything* about where they come from secret. It's like, something out of fantasy. No wonder you and your father love Lord of the Rings so much. Though, there are zero girls in it."

"Not zero," I said, sweeping in like a knight to protect the book I'd given her as a sacred gift a year earlier.

"I know, I know. Almost. I wanted more about Eowyn and Galadriel and those ladies. But more than that, I want to know more about your grandpa and grandma and what they got up to."

"Me too," I smiled.

Sitting there in my family's library, with the early evening light slanting in through the wooden slats of the great shuttered windows, our sock-clad heels against the cool iron oxide floor, I wanted more than anything to show Alice *my culture*. To show her what I myself didn't quite know, in the shadow of great wings stirring just out of sight.

"Do you really not know where your family's from? Like, even your distant ancestors? Or do you just pretend with strangers because it's top secret?"

"You're not a stranger. Do you know a lot about Chinese culture?"

"Not a *lot* lot. We go to the Chinese churches and all sometimes, even though Mamma's not religious. When I was younger we'd go on these family trips to the temple in Achipur, and have picnics by the river, that was nice. They say that was where the first Chinese guy ended up here. His grave is there. I know how to say some things in Hakka. But I don't know it like Bangla and English. My Chinese grandparents are always scolding me for forgetting where I'm from. But I'm from Cal only. Then there's your parents who don't even tell you where you're from. Total opposite. Or do they? You didn't say."

"They don't. I really don't know. Just that our ancestors were nomads and moved around all the time."

"Hmm," Alice raised a leg on to the sofa, hammering her chin against her bare knee like it was an anvil. "Did you know that my father lived in this house for a bit?"

"What? No way."

"Yeah. My parents told me, when I started coming here. It was way before we were born. When India and China had a war. In the '60s, I think. The government was sending Chinese people here to these prison camps or back to China, and taking away their houses, because they thought we were all spies. Your family took in my father's family, hid them I guess. I don't know how or why, they were pretty vague. But they lived here for a few years. That's probably why they set up the restaurant here."

"I had no idea."

Alice looked at me. "We're almost like family," she said softly. I didn't feel like she was, but I did feel an incredible debt of gratitude to my family right then. There she was, sitting beside me with her chin nocked on her knee, because of something they did decades ago.

~5~

A MEMORY: MY grandmother kneeling in front of the shrine in the corner of her bedroom, incense smoke scribbling the air and sweetening it. The shrine was simple, just a low wooden table with the portrait of my grandfather from the library on it, smaller and in a tin frame, carefully positioned in the centre of a lace doily. A brass incense holder next to the photo, and a scroll hung on the wall, like the ones Maa had shown me when she took off her headscarf. Didima was whispering words to my grandfather's picture. She looked at me watching her, after a long silence.

"Come," she said. I sat down cross-legged next to her, looking at the beautiful face in the photo.

"You don't know anything about your grandfather, na?" she said, stroking my unruly hair, which was neither short nor long. I shook my head. This wasn't long after I left school, and I had stopped getting haircuts at the barber's.

"You're bored at home all the time, I can tell. Do you want to know a secret that shouldn't be a secret?"

I nodded.

"You've had lunch? And the halahala?"

I nodded.

"Good. Then I will tell you, and you will forget. But keep it in your heart. You're maybe too young to hear this story," she reached out to touch the photo lightly. "But why not, hm? You will forget. You know about boys and girls, babu?" I wasn't sure what she meant by that, but I nodded. I was twelve, had some idea about sex, and was vaguely panicked by the idea that my grandmother might talk to me about it when my parents hadn't.

"There's that saying they have here," she said, whether or not I was ready. "'They were too good for this world.' I don't know, maybe that's just silly. But with your grandfather, I wonder." When she spoke next, it was in the fire tongue.

"But listen. Your grandfather was a woman when I met them first. We were drawn to each other. What you call love in English, prem in Bangla. When we knew that we wanted to be together, we decided we wanted a child. So we asked the serpent," my grandmother looked up at the scroll above my grandfather's portrait, the script on it twisting and coiling behind the incense smoke.

"The serpent knows no gender nor sex. A dragon may spring from the world tree, or lay the egg that grows the tree, or simply live forever, if time and space allow. It may decide to mate with one or many other serpents, or dance alone. Any dragon, no matter what kind or what size, given time and desire, can become the Queen that lays the egg, with or without mates. The seed that spawns dragons is dream. That is why the serpent binds to us, frail and mortal, despite its power—for our dreams. For that it shares its aspect, its wealth, its wisdom, with us, if we respect it.

"Your grandfather and I slept naked in the great tent of the serpent's wings, the only temple we have ever known, under the heat and light of its maw, arm in arm in a river of our sweat and blood as it wove its web around us. When we woke, my beloved was still a woman, but also a man…n iayu lx. The same person, dreamed anew. And then my beloved and I had an infant child together, and I carried her in me on the back of the serpent as it bore us to distant shores of reality. Our child became your Maa. I miss your grandfather very much. I wish they had lasted longer in this world."

She looked at me. "You understood?"

I felt like I had understood something. I knew gods and goddesses changed from man to woman and woman to man, in the myths I read about. I thought it was strange and beautiful that my grandmother looked at my grandfather this way. Not for the first time, I wondered where it was in the world beyond Calcutta that they had slept in the tented temple that she referred to as a dragon's wings—an image out of the books my father collected.

"This world has forgotten many things. Now you can forget this also," my grandmother murmured. I didn't want to, I wanted to keep my eyes on the steepled wings of a dragon reaching to the misted sky, walking under their arches hand in hand with someone to re-dream myself into someone, instead of a boy from nowhere. But forget I did, for a time.

I don't know how many stories my grandmother seeded in me over the years, right before the fog of forgetfulness rolled in.

ALICE AND I, caught in torrential monsoon rain, shoulder to shoulder under my umbrella in the narrow alleyways around Central Avenue, their gutters overflowing and footpaths nonexistent. Feet and socks wet inside our shoes, sloshing through the brown waters, we reached a footpath with our soles squelching. I bent the umbrella, water pearling off its edges, low over our heads. The rain drummed frantic over our heads. "We're under a dragon's wing," I shouted over the rain, as we walked towards the direction of the Chens' place. "It'll shelter us all the way home."

"Tell the dragon to open its wings wider, what is it, a baby?" she said, as the ground shattered the rain against us. "Ow," she said, as the skeleton under the wing snagged in her hair as I held the umbrella too low. My apologies were profuse. "It's okay, I'm fine, really. Your dragon doesn't like me," she said, laughing in the silvery light.

~6~

I STARTED MAKING the short walk to the Chens' flat more frequently. Crammed together on the same bed, we'd browse the internet on their dial-up modem and play games on their family computer with Alice's intimidating older brother Francis, who thrashed me to pixellated smears of blood when playing the latest Mortal Kombat, and called me a girl less kindly than his sister. Alice defended me valiantly in our little tournaments, tongue tucked against a corner of her mouth, making the bed groan and shake as she danced with the controller, putting up fierce fights against her 'baka-boka' brother for my honour on the little CRT window to another world. He usually beat her too, even playing on the keyboard, but not as often as me. Alice standing up for me didn't extend to our own battles, in which she defeated me handily.

We used Alice's library card for the British Council Library on Shakespeare Sarani, where O and A level exams for her school were held, and borrowed movies to watch on the Chens' big TV and VCR when her parents were out at the restaurant. Out of some familiar instinct, I looked for dragons on the hefty plastic cassette covers, but none had any, so I settled on fantastical movies like *Highlander* and *Conan the Barbarian* (Alice and Francis enjoyed the horror movies more than me, though she screamed often). Francis guided our borrowing with a deft hand, introducing us to all manner of gore and nudity. We felt uncomfortably mature watching 'dirty scenes' in silence instead of nervously laughing like at first, less so when Francis called us perverted children. I felt undeniably guilty when, later in my own room, these sex scenes and my togetherness with Alice during them formed the backdrop of my adolescent onanistic discoveries.

When we weren't watching movies or having virtual tests of strength with her brother, Alice would drag me into her room. After abusing Francis mercilessly in his presence, she once assured me later: "Francis isn't as much of a doofus as he seems." It's true that Francis was nicer when he played guitar for us, or demonstrated his metal growl using Alice's hairbrush as a mic. "You know he actually lets me win at Mortal Kombat. He's too good to lose. He goes at you because he thinks you're going to be my boyfriend and he has to be a good big brother and scare you into not breaking my heart."

"What," I gasped, as if such a thought had never struck me in all the years, and had dropped like a stone on my head. "That's. Not. I'm not your boyfriend," I said.

Alice laughed. "Duh. My brother is okay, but he's a dimwit."

"I would never break your heart," I blurted out.

Alice took the stuffed pig next to her on the bed, and placed it in her lap like a puppy. "You're sweet," she said, as if to the pig, and looked at me. "But you don't know that, no one does," she said, looking wiser than her years. I felt a little frightened by her thought, if also vaguely empowered.

Alice's room was cramped, but had a little verandah adjoining it. We sat there with our limbs through the metal grill, legs dangling over the street. The little space was filled with the clean scent of drying laundry on the clotheslines strung across it, dripping on our backs. When her girl friends were there, we'd be packed in there like monkeys in a cage, I the only boy. They treated me like Alice's strange little step-brother they had to babysit, even though I was their age—not ignoring me, exactly, but talking around me about their intricate social dramas. Alice would look nervous, and ask if I was bored. But I didn't mind, so they didn't either. They were endlessly entertained by tying my hair into pigtails or braids (sloppier than the ones Maa and Baba tied). Some days I even absorbed their enthusiasm, joining them as they goaded each other into shooting spitballs at passing pedestrians or bursting into song (only partially imitating them when it was Bollywood songs, since my Hindi was terrible), our audience down below gaping up at us without ever stopping, the street dogs occasionally howling along. On the Lunar New Year, the street below Alice's verandah became a river of people parted by the path of dancing lions and dragons. We watched their neon-bright manes and frilled scales twirl down below to the beat of drums, our bare feet hanging down through the grill and over the heads of the spectators to tempt the snapping jaws of the beasts. They never bit.

On drowsy summer afternoons Alice and I sat there for hours with her Discman between our thighs, earphone wires stretched between our heads, one bud each so we could still talk about books, movies, the ongoing soap opera of her school life. When she was feeling especially vulnerable, she let slip a crush or two on boys in her class, though they never seemed to lead anywhere. These conversations would still pain me with irrepressible jealousy, and gladden me with the knowledge that she trusted me. I preferred when she settled on the topic of her more famous crushes, like her favourites Shahrukh Khan, Keanu Reeves and Leonardo DiCaprio (I'd gone to see *Titanic* with Alice and her friends, and remember the chorus of sighs across our row when the first glimpse of the actor's eyes in close-up flitted across the screen—Alice had a *Titanic* poster on the door of her room). She would even confide in me about her period pains, which made me immensely proud, as if I were an honorary handmaiden to her.

Sometimes it would just be the music in our ears playing to the whir of Alice's warming Discman, as the narrow valley of the street shifted blue with evening and the streetlights turned on, the crows cawing and our arms mosquito-welted to signal coming darkness, at which point Auntie Chen would shout at us from the living room to join everyone for tea and Alice would shout back to bring it to the verandah. There and then, the storm that roiled always in me, rising and falling but never going away, fanned by great wings unseen, by the lashing of serpents, calmed to something imperceptible, and I would look up at the setting sun soaking the edges of the rooftops like a normal boy sitting next to a friend he had come to love.

~1~

IN THE LATE 1970S, before I was born, my father met an American named Sam Walsh. He often came to eat and read pulp paperbacks at the Crystal Dragon. Sam stood out because of his whiteness, his heft, and a limp he said he'd acquired in Vietnam as a war correspondent, which led him to retire and seek the dubious peace of India. But it was those fascinating paperbacks with dragons on the covers that drew Baba to Sam. Once they broke the ice over drinks, Baba welcomed this gregarious, bearded American into the Dragoners Club. Baba and him would often smoke up and listen to records at the club while talking about science fiction and fantasy. Like many of the white tourists who frequented the city at the time, he had sought out Calcutta for its hashish and spiritual allure. Sam (as my parents referred to him) was one of the few people allowed inside our home, though only in specific parts. He loved the Club's food and dragon décor, its charming secrecy, Baba's library. He only got the normal stuff—no 'whole dragon' platters. I don't know if Sam was given the Tea of Forgetfulness, but he never brought anyone else to the Club, and didn't seem to have any other close friends in Calcutta.

My parents didn't have any friends outside of our 'people' either, so Sam was unique. He would vanish to America for months on end, but always came back, looking more disheveled than before. I wasn't born when he'd become Baba's pal, but I did grow up with him as a kind of foreign uncle. He'd bring me back Hershey's chocolate bars that I thought smelled a bit of vomit but tasted delicious, packs of Wrigley's spearmint gum that I chewed until my jaws ached, and tubes of Pringles that I hoarded like every chip was a gold piece, rationing them and getting angry when the adults stole a few. But as I grew older, I appreciated the collections he added to my father's library more than the foreign snacks—comic books and novels that were hard to find in India at the time, and shiny video cassettes of all kinds of movies that weren't the pirated copies with colour Xerox covers we got at Verdaan or A.C. Market. Baba's library of science fiction and fantasy expanded exponentially because of Sam. I loved when Sam appeared at our home because of these gifts, because it meant going out with him and Baba and Maa to the nearby Broadway Hotel, Sam's Calcuttan abode. I happily ate my breaded fish fry and undercooked French fries with a big pungent puddle of kasundi and ketchup, while Sam and Baba got drunk on endless beers (Maa partook as well, but never as much), their laughter rising to the high ceilings and rattling fans of the bar as if it were an ancient banquet hall, the cigarette smoke haze fumes from a nonexistent fireplace. Sam did always look to me, with his beard and his broadness, like an oversized Dwarf, like he belonged in the fictions he enthusiastically discussed with Baba. Of course, it was us, my family and me, who truly belonged in worlds such as those, something I knew somewhere deep down in myself, but not with any certainty back then.

Once Baba finished the fantasy novel manuscript he'd been hammering out on his typewriter for so many years, he shared it with Sam. Sam loved it, loved the very idea of an Indian fellow of Baba's ethnically ambiguous looks (Baba identified us as 'atheists', giving Sam the impression that we were New Agers philosophically opposed to being identified by our ethnicity, though he probably assumed we were Chinese Indian) writing an English language fantasy novel. Baba's book was about dragon-riders on a distant world migrating through space using their steeds' ability to traverse multiple realities. The reason; empires on their world destroying themselves by the exploitation of dragons as world-breaking weapons and reality-weavers. In the end, the nomads and their dragons find Earth, of course. Sam would talk about how it reminded him of Superman ('Escape from dragon Krypton!') and Anne McCaffrey while coughing on his overstuffed spliffs. He told Baba he was starting a publishing company back in Seattle, and would make him famous.

I was very young at the time, but I remember my parents fighting furiously over Sam's proposed book deal. Maa tolerated Sam and even enjoyed his company sometimes, but felt he was trying to take advantage of my father, that there was a reason they didn't go around making friends in Calcutta, let alone perpetually stoned hippies from America. Once, Baba shouted, "I'm doing it to honour you, your mother, our family." Maa said, "Please! You're *using* us to honour yourself and try and become famous like those authors you read all day. You're selling our culture to a man we don't even know anything about!" I am of course piecing together these arguments from what I can make of the situation in retrospect, from the words I heard flying between the two of them. But young as I was, I understood that Baba wanted to publish his book, and that Maa didn't want him to.

Despite my mother's protests, my father ultimately signed the contract. As a compromise that my mother probably didn't ask for, he used a ridiculous pseudonym that he and Sam came up with during one of their hash-smoking sessions as a tribute to some of both of their favourite authors. Surprisingly, the deal wasn't a con. Sam left Calcutta for a year and came back one day with two paperback copies of *The Dragoner's Daughter*. The cover was a garishly painted portrait of a tanned, green-eyed woman in a metal bikini brandishing a blade on a sinewy emerald dragon, its wings unfurled and ablaze in the light of a star rising over the crescent of a blue planet. Baba wasn't especially pleased by this choice of artwork for his lyrical novel about a clan of dragoners leaving a war-torn world, but went along with it. I remember him pathetically trailing my mother, trying to show her the book.

The Last Dragoners of Bowbazar

She glanced at it, her face stone, and went on with the chores she was doing without a word. He showed it to me with great pride. When I asked if it was like *The Hobbit* but with a girl, he laughed. He held my hand and took me with him to show the book to his mother. She was using her spinning wheel to weave what must have been the invisible silk headscarves. My grandmother looked at the book with a squint, and gave it back to my father. "If this is how you show respect to our people, you are very foolish," she said. I looked up at Baba. I'd never seen him look so ill.

XORAAL WATCHES THE young dragon leap off his arm and take first flight, the gauntlet on his arm no longer weighed down by its heavy black talons.

He has done this so many times, but it always makes him smile when they soar for the first time, their wings unfurling on the freezing winds like sun-drenched flags. Xoraal looks at Shoxia, who watches in awe as the dragon flies from her father. She looks every bit his daughter, an even younger drake sitting on her shoulder.

The drake twitches its growing wings, as if in imitation of its elder in the sky.

EXCERPT, THE DRAGONER'S DAUGHTER BY ELRIC RAY KROEBER (SPEARPOINT PRESS, TPB PUB. 1988)

~2~

THE DRAGONER'S DAUGHTER was Spearpoint Press's first and only book, and sold about fifty-two copies. "Too much like Anne McCaffrey," Sam mused over Old Monk at the Crystal Dragon. Baba got two royalty statements (both for 0 dollars or rupees) from Seattle before they stopped coming. He did get an advance for the book. I never found out how much it was. I can't imagine it was very much. Sam's small press closed down in a year or so. The remaining copies of the novel were pulped.

Sam Walsh disappeared from Calcutta (or perhaps just from our lives) soon after the failure of my father's book and the publishing company. This was a while before the days of the internet, and we never saw him again. I often think of Uncle Sam, who hated to be called that, having come away from his time in Vietnam with a mellow but undying anti-authoritarian mistrust of his country. I think of the gifts he brought me, and his destiny as the herald of my father's short-lived fiction career on Earth. After Sam stopped showing up at our home every so often like a fickle wizard between mysterious quests, I'd ask Baba about him. Baba always shrugged and said, "It's getting more expensive to travel all the way here from America," and dismissed his dear friend's memory like an annoyance. I learned to stop asking. I don't know if Baba ever secretly corresponded with Sam after the whole mess with the book, or at least received a letter explaining the disappearance. I still hope that it was shame that kept

Sam from seeing us again, and not a darker fate beyond the collapse of his dream business.

In the aftermath of the book's failure to soar alongside the science-fiction and fantasy classics he'd lined our shelves with, I would often see him sitting in the garden, pretending to read his own book. He'd stop every few seconds to shake his head and look at the cover, as if questioning the folly he was holding in his hands. Then he'd stand with his hand against the trunk of the great tree in the centre of the garden, whispering something into the bark with his eyes closed. I watched from afar, from the balconies. One of those dusks, Maa came to join him, putting her hand on his shoulder as he sat under the tree and stared at his failed book. He looked up, surprised. She sat next to him on the ground. He looked like a cornered cat as she patted his arm and said something. He turned so his back faced her.

With infinite tenderness, I saw my mother gather my father's long, uncombed black locks in her hands and tie them into a neat braid. They sat together for a while as the dusk deepened, Baba holding the book in his hands. His mouth moved, and she listened. He was reading to her. The bats came out of the trees to bring in the coming dark.

SAM TOOK THE original manuscript of my father's novel with him to Seattle when they'd first signed the contract. Baba burned the two paperback copies we had, lighting a kerosene fire in the courtyard garden when he was drunk. Maa stamped it out. She saved one of the copies that got less of a sprinkle of fuel, just about—much of it was blackened. I never got to read the entire thing. The burnt, salvaged copy was stored in an ornate wooden box in the library like a cursed tome, but not very securely. As the weight of my family's impossibility weighs heavier with each passing day, I wish I could have read the entire thing.

But many years after Baba's little bonfire, Alice and I did open that box, with its carven lid and ashy smell. We read the parts of *The Dragoner's Daughter* we could, carefully handling the crumbling book like the rare collector's item it was (if only any collectors knew about it). Alice and I would sit on the rooftop terrace and read the fire-stained passages to each other under the open sky, my father downstairs, completely oblivious to his new fans. I remember the glimpses in prose of a giant world where there was no ground, only an eternal ocean of storms and gaseous seas, where nomads lived in the sky in huts woven from the silken spit of serpents, in cities strung like dewdrops across webs suspended between the branches of primordial world trees, their trunks endless and roots lost to the depths, higher than the highest mountains on Earth, from which dragons grew, and in which dragons lived. How great empires that had grown like barnacles on the trunks and branches of the mountainous world trees began to infect the minds of their serpents to reflect their avarice, turning them rage-filled and vast, howling weapons to warp reality and raze rival clans, filling all the skies with war and tearing the branches of the world trees asunder for the first time in millennia. How the nomads planned their escape from the world, forced to flee with their own dragons to find peace, hounded across realities by the hateful winged legions of evil empires. How they swam endless through the multi-real oceans of spacetime, looking for a new world to shelter them.

Beyond the timeless canyons of cosmic megastructures and through the fractal filaments of spacetime, into another universe and down a spiral staircase of stars, a pale blue dot beckoning.

~1~

IT WAS THE YEAR Alice Chen and I saw the first *Lord of the Rings* movie at New Empire (I went again with Baba, who hugged me after, overcome) that we kissed, as was inevitable, or only so in hindsight. It was that very day, in fact—my eighteenth birthday, the day she surprised me with pre-booked matinee tickets for the two of us, and held my hand in the light-lanced dark as Sam and Frodo embraced in a boat.

Afterward, she came back to the house with me. Fired up by the movie, Alice wanted more knowledge of the strange and fantastical lore of our family, the scarce glimpses of which over the years had given us a shared language of yearning, like the books we read together. Baba, who had wanted to hear all about the movie, was excited by the opportunity to show off like the old days, since the Dragoners Club was getting emptier by the day. He invited Alice to early dinner at the canteen for the first time in all the years of her knowing my family, swapping out our birthday tradition of meeting at the Crystal Dragon. Alice, sick as always of the food there, was fine with this, calling her parents to let them know she'd be home later.

Maa was surprisingly warm and receptive to the presence of Alice in this forbidden space. Perhaps my stunt of bringing classmates in there so many years ago had prepared her for the inevitability of Alice one day entering the inner sanctum. But I knew she was fond of Alice too, always had been, in spite of her wariness of anyone beyond the walls of the house. I think she was secretly glad for the rare opportunity to sit down and have a meal with her son's single true friend. In any case, the meal was less shocking than the one Neil and Ranjan blundered into years ago. My parents brought in steamed rice, and a kadai of mutton stew so spicy it burned in our nostrils before we'd even taken a bite. "Dragon Roast Mutton," announced Baba.

Alice peered at the kadai. "That smells delicious, Auntie and Uncle, but why does it sound like something out of our menu downstairs?" she laughed.

"She's going to do all that oriental this-that talk now, just you see. Paka meye," said Maa, patting her shoulder and sitting down.

Baba was delighted. "It's a simple, factual name, Alice. I promise you this isn't Indian Chinese or anything you've had before. It's our people's food, like you wanted. First, you bring a live goat to the center of the dragon's nest—let's say, this house—and you anoint it with song, and blood from your arm," he held out his forearm, where there was a pale scar. Maa was looking a bit uncomfortable now. "The dragon presents itself. Its wings sweep the sky. Folded above you," my father paused, as if choosing his words carefully. "It's like standing under the arches of a cathedral. Humbled, you ask the dragon to give its blessing. The dragon licks the sacrificial goat with a tongue of flame as pure as the sun. For just an instant, no longer. We peel the crispy black skin off that dead goat with our blades, scoop out the scorching entrails, all given to the serpent. The meat melts off the bones, easy. We use that sanctified flesh, seasoned with dragon's breath, to cook this stew. Hence, Dragon Roast Mutton. Simple." Baba smiled, bearing the look of a magician who had explained a trick. I had a vision unbidden of my mother's arm straining as she held a rope leash tight and walked a goat back home from the Muslim butcher nearby, me following at a safe distance, having been butted by more than one of the sacrificial animals and sent sprawling.

"That is so cool, Uncle. Can't wait to try it," said Alice, who was clearly thinking of my father's short writing career. I'd forbidden her to mention this because the topic made him touchy. Maa's shoulders slumped a bit, and she smiled. Of course there was nothing to believe here. Stories were stories. Alice knew this. We ate the stew with rice, the flavor smoky, violently hot—the meat succulent and soft, with a sharp, juicy iron tang that reminded me only of blood. "It's so good, Uncle, Auntie," said Alice, face flushed and slick with sweat. She finished everything on her plate. Seeing her struggle with the spice, Baba went to the fridge and brought a chilled bottle of Kingfisher to the table, and poured it into two glasses.

"Why not, you're both old enough for a bit of beer," he said, looking at Maa for implicit permission. "Don't drink it all in one go, you two. I don't want to be explaining to your parents why we allowed their daughter to get drunk," Maa said, smiling at Alice. Alice grinned at this reserved acknowledgment of our maturity. "Cheers," said Baba, raising his own glass of whiskey. "To Ru and Alice, on the cusp of adulthood, and to the little clans forged around dinner tables." Despite the warmth inside and outside our bodies, I shivered as we all said *cheers* and clashed our glasses together.

After the heavy mutton and our enthusiastic sips of beer, we had more trouble finishing the pungent fish porridge that was served after. Baba said it was "coaxed from the belly of a serpent sent to the sky to seek its fellow moon-spurred snake, the Hooghly, and burrow into her fleshy waters, to return with silver bounty." *Dragon vomit*, I thought. "You send a drake of the air fishing when the sky is overcast, so it can slip in and out of hiding, during monsoon and kalboishaki, so it may ride the rain and wind, and any hapless bystander under an umbrella will see a lash of lightning strike the river rather than a serpent bright." Alice laughed and clapped.

I had eaten all of this before, yet the stories rang in my head like I was only hearing them, the memories vibrating alongside—my mother caressing the spiky, metallic shape coiled around her in the cloud-darkened courtyard, a slurry of boiling silvered slime thrumming into a huge cast iron dekchi on the floor from steaming jaws opened over her shoulder. The dripping, jet black umbrella protecting her from a pattering rain not an umbrella at all, too large, too misshapen, the quivering wings of the serpent wrapped around her.

"This one's more of an acquired taste, no doubt," Baba said. "We add lots of rice to make it less...powerful. The rice cooks by itself, no flame, nothing, because the base is so hot."

"It's amazing. Just really full from the mutton," Alice said bravely, taking small spoonfuls.

At the end of the meal, I said to my parents, "Don't give us the Tea of Forgetfulness."

"Wait, that sounds interesting. I wanna have that," said Alice. My parents exchanged glances.

"No you don't, it's disgusting and bitter. Like cough syrup. Trust me," I said.

"But what if I tell people all your cooking secrets are down to dragons?" said Alice, narrowing her eyes and hunching her head like a villain.

"Oh, come now, we know you'd never betray us, beta," said Baba flamboyantly to slacken the tension creeping into the air, glancing at Maa. "I think we're out of the tea anyway," she said, and started clearing the table. Alice mimed zipping her mouth, oblivious. "Your secret's safe with me, Uncle." Nothing further was said about the tea. Perhaps there was nothing really for us to forget, but it was the first time my parents had ever agreed not to give me the halahala.

ALICE AND I helped my parents wash the dishes in the canteen, and went upstairs to the rooftop terrace to watch the sun set. On the way up, we said hello to my grandmother, who was napping in her room as she often did now. She asked for a hug from us both and let us go on up. Alice was fidgety, still flushed from the meal, though it was no whole dragon platter. I could see that my father's descriptions had brought her a little of the way into the truth of the house. Her intense, renewed curiosity further uncoiled part of all that was suppressed in my own body and mind of that same truth, and of my dependence on her normal self. Up on the terrace, the sky was cloudless above, a vast river between the garden of my house on one side, and the city on the other, its many windows burning with the setting sun.

Alice leaned over the smog-stained wall of the terrace on the side that looked over the courtyard garden. The top of the tree in the centre extended beyond our eye level, the capillary branches of its crown filtering silhouette black into the sky. Wings fluttered in the dim, wheeling around its boughs.

"I can see the little dragons flying around the tree," said Alice, rearing her head to the breeze that rustled the treetop, letting it cool her damp face. I squinted at the winged shapes streaking across the smoulder of sunset. They looked like bats to me. The garden was twinkling with dancing lights as it gathered shadows in preparation for night.

"Look, so pretty. Those aren't fireflies. It's the littlest dragons, the size of mosquitoes, like in your father's book. They don't like the pollution in Cal. They're doing chotto coughs of fire. Kawaii," she said, squeaking the last word and scratching her arm. "Biting me too."

She took my hand, the second time that day, and pulled me away from the wall. "Lie down with me," she said, letting go of my hand and lying flat on the ground. She was wearing a dark floral cami dress over a Slipknot T-shirt her brother had given her for her birthday a few months earlier, a black lace choker coiled around her neck. I assumed her dress was new too, I'd never seen her wear it.

"Your clothes'll get dirty."

"Seriously?" she asked from down on the ground. I untied my hair and lay down next to her, the sides of our arms touching. I slipped my green scrunchie around my wrist, the same one she'd given me years ago. It had grown slack, and had to be tied a few more times than before.

Alice drummed on her stomach with her palms, letting out a soft burp. "Oh my god, so full. Your parents are crazy cooks."

I placed my hands on my own belly, feeling a bit queasy.

"What's with you, why so quiet? You were talking non-stop after the movie. Is something wrong?" asked Alice.

"No, no. Just birthday thoughts."

"Hmm. Being an adult sucks for sure. Welcome to year eighteen," she said, as if she'd been eighteen forever instead of a few months. I'd gone to her party at the Chens' flat. Lost in a sea of in-jokes among her classmates, including the once-mysterious boys who were far less interested in Alice's quiet neighbour than her girl friends, I'd also left early. Alice had looked disappointed.

"I was thinking that you'll be done with school next year," I said.

"I'm the one who should be sad about that, not you. You're just thinking about how much you're going to miss hanging out with my girl friends, aren't you?"

"Shut up."

"Don't worry, I'll still call them over when you're around. Just for you. Including Neha, who still has a crush on you, by the way."

"She does not."

"Oh-kay," Alice laughed. "You can be such a clueless prettyhead sometimes."

Like a talisman she was drawn to, she took my hand again, and held it up a bit, gently brushing her thumb over my knuckles, the nearly invisible scar there. She knew it was there.

"From when I punched a racist. In the ancient days when *I* was in school," I said. She knew the story too.

"Pretty tough guy behaviour for a beautiful princess from a mysterious culture."

"Princesses can be tough."

She laughed in exasperation. "I know, Ru, there's nothing wrong with being a girl blahdi blah. You don't have to impress me all the time. I know you're wise. But I like that you're soft." She placed my hand back on my stomach. I turned to look at her in the fading light, to see if she was annoyed. I couldn't tell.

"I don't think we even had princesses in our culture," I said.

"True, none in your father's book. Fine, so you're not a princess. Just beautiful," I could hear the smile in her words. "Like Arwen in the movie. Except not white. Arwen does become a queen later, though. You can't escape your fate."

The sky was bisected by the empty clothesline above us, stretched across the terrace on poles. The golden embers of sunset we'd seen piled up against the dark skyline of Calcutta were going out, sparking the stars, if only the ones that shone bright enough across the aeons to pierce the thin scum of smog above this little patch of Earth. The beacon of an aircraft crawled among them, a soothing rumble. Alice stood up abruptly, brushing her dress off and grabbing the clothesline with her hands. I got up too. She pulled on the line, looking up at the stars, at the frosty fingerprint of a three-quarter moon against the cloudless pane of the sky. "Sometimes I still can't believe this is real," she breathed.

"What is?"

"That I'm friends with you. Like, full-on the last of your kind. I remember when I thought you were just this weird kid who didn't go to school and lived somewhere above ma-baba's restaurant. Little did I know you hold the secrets of an entire world."

I rasped my sneakers across the ground. "Not a kid, but I am still that."

"Don't look down, look up." I did. She tugged on the clothesline again, pulling it down with her body weight. "This is the cord of spit spun from a dragon's maw, across the sky. The invisible dragon's web that dragoners know to see," she said, paraphrasing, pulling words from *The Dragoner's Daughter*. "There's no ground under us. And that up there is the eternal ocean. Don't let go, you might fall forever around the worlds."

"I thought we were adults now. Year eighteen and all that."

She let go of the clothesline so it bounced and hummed. "Not very mysterious of you."

"Stop calling—I'm not mysterious. At least, I don't want to be. And you know all this…dragon worship talk, that isn't real, right? My father just made all that up."

Alice looked at me and wiped her forehead, her buoyant body language gone. "Why are you talking to me like I'm stupid?" Her voice was sharp. She turned away from me and walked across the terrace to the boundary wall on the other side, looking out to the city. I followed.

"Alice?"

"I thought we were having fun. I had such an awesome day with you, and. What the fuck do you even mean? Did you think watching the Lord of the Rings made me think there are hobbits hiding in your family garden? Of course I know it isn't real. Nothing is. On Chinese New Year the dragons aren't real, doesn't mean you can't have fun watching them. Don't we? I thought that's what we were doing."

I walked to her side. She moved away. I stepped back. We had never really fought. If we got annoyed with each other, we usually just recognized it and stayed apart for a while. I wondered if that was healthy. I wondered if I had just ruined our friendship.

"I'm sorry," I said. She didn't say anything.

"I know it sounds weird, me asking that," I continued. "I forgot how weird because it's you. But the fact is, I *don't* know what's real, sometimes. Whether my family's from this country, or nowhere, or what. I don't know how it's possible to have a culture that no one in the world seems to have heard of. I don't know who...my 'people' are, or who I should be. I don't feel like I'm Indian, or what a man is supposed to be, or even human, some days."

Alice turned from the city to me, the moon in her eyes dancing.

"It does feel like I'm the last of my kind," I said. "It doesn't feel good, it feels like time's running out and I'm doing nothing, am nothing. I don't even know what my legacy is, what I'm supposed to remember and honour. I get confused. And, and I have no way of describing it to anyone. No one has the words. I have no one to tell. Except you.

"I know you're real," I said.

"I *am* stupid," she said, soft.

"No, you're not."

"I am. I didn't even think. Your family, you, you're all so sweet to me that I didn't even think about what it might be like for you. I was just playing around and it's your whole... life I was playing with. I'm so stupid."

"You're not. I overreacted. It's okay."

"No. It's not. It's not," she moved towards me, taking my face in her warm hands. "It will be. You'll be okay." She leaned forward and pressed her mouth gently against my cheek. "Oh, Ru, I didn't realize, I'm so sorry." I closed my eyes, and her lips were on mine, our tongues touching, a sour hint of dragon's breath in our throats as our heartbeats met. We separated, her hands against my neck, and I stared disbelieving at her face washed in dusk, her hair clinging to her forehead, quivering in the breeze.

"That was my first kiss," I told her.

"Mine too," she said, pulling me close so our bodies touched. She wrapped her arms around me in a tight hug, face nestled against my neck. I shivered as she spoke against my skin. "Ru?"

"Yeah?"

"You know you can talk to me, right?"

We broke our hug, arms still around each other. "Yeah," I said, looking into her gleaming eyes. "I do. All the time."

"You know what I mean. I'd never tell anyone about the things I learn here, with you. You can tell me when you feel confused, or...not normal. You're not alone. I've felt it so many times, in school, in this city, when I walk around and people stare and I think, is it because I'm Chinese or because I'm a girl. I think feeling that way makes you pretty normal, you know?"

"Thanks," I said, looking away from her face, which felt too bright, somehow, after our kiss. A breath released in laughter, and her hand on my chest. "Not too normal, obviously. That's boring." Her hand came up to my face, ever so light against my cheek to turn my face back to her.

"You exist," she said.

The Last Dragoners of Bowbazar

A KISS AT eighteen, under a March moon waxing gibbous, the world tree shimmering just out of sight, airplanes among the stars watching us in envy. Afterward, I took Alice to rooms she had never entered before in the house, the ones that guests never went to but weren't locked. My parents were down in the club room drinking, and my grandmother was asleep, and I knew that she wouldn't care anyway. Because it was my birthday, we knew Alice's parents were unlikely to call and ask her to come home until later in the night, so we had time to do our own thing for a while. The upper stories of the house were empty, labyrinthine in the fresh dark. So Alice and I explored.

I took her to the room with parchment on the walls, crawling with dense language that wavered like flame and coiled like sinew under our gaze, where my mother had first shown me her headscarf. If we looked long enough, we could see faint tributaries in the leathery parchment, like trees or rivers or networks of capillaries that had once flowed with life.

I took her to the room with tapestries of silk so fine they were translucent, the rippling serpents and flames on them almost vanishing like tricks of the light. One of the tapestries, almost covering an entire wall, showed a solar system not our own, the interlocking circles of celestial spheres glittering on their spiderweb-fine weave.

I took her to the room full of cupboards lined with curved daggers of black and white bone behind glass panes, some fashioned into actual bladed weapons and some bare, others threaded with string or wire to become jewelry. Teeth and claws, small as droplets of pearl, long and curved as scimitars. Jagged shards of flickering, multi-hued glass—or the chipped scales of something vast. We didn't open the locked cupboards—just stood and observed it all in reverent silence, Alice's face childlike with wonder. We didn't speak to each other about what animal's bones those scales and fangs and claws might be carved from, or what mineral or stone. We let them be, as they were. We wandered back out onto the verandahs and looked through the clotheslines to the glistening garden and its great tree swathed in night, which sang with insects, frogs, things unknown. "Can we read from the book?" asked Alice, and I knew instantly what she meant.

So we went into the familiar haunt of the library to sneak the damaged copy of *The Dragoner's Daughter* from its box, along with a bottle of Old Monk from the liquor cabinet (at Alice's nervously excited suggestion), and we went back upstairs to the roof to take turns reading aloud by the light of a torch. I disliked the taste of the rum on my tongue from our judicious sips, but thrilled at its bittersweetness on Alice's mouth when we kissed again between the words we read. Small dragons wheeled up above squeaking like bats, their wings pale in starlight. We lay on the ground next to each other and hung off the Earth, and we were not on Earth, but dragoners on the void reaches above the world of eternal storm, where ocean and sky were churned into one by the great serpents when time was young. Sky above and below, we were nomads on the invisible lattice of the dragons' web, strung from the titanic branches of a world tree that reaches down forever into the abyssal blue, down through the topmost calms of vapour and cloud, through superionic seas and volatile ice, through blazing storms and diamond rains that forever prism the lightning, to the burning core where the nebular serpents that danced the primordial dirt of the void into a sphere of space and time that became the world, dance still among the flaming roots of this planetary grove. Hand in hand, Alice and I saw above us the night side of this world so vast it would fill the entire sky of Earth. We felt our bodies lighten, our hands clasped tight to stay together lest we fall into its enormous gravity. We saw the lights of distant cities and villages glittering on the invisible dragon's web like stars, suspended above (below) us against the dark blue of the eternal ocean, its deceptive calm hiding tidal winds that would tear us limb from limb. We saw the bright and luminous sphere of a woven dragon's hive hovering like a moon in the invisible web, the construct of a dragoner empire, far vaster than any of the starry clan cities it dwarfed. We saw far below us as we hung from our own small, insignificant nest like a speck of dew-wrapped dust on the web, a telltale flicker of phosphorescence clinging to the shadow of a dragon sailing the eternal ocean on outstretched wings, its breath a spear of light to herald its path, its roar echoing between the worlds.

~2~

TIME WILL TURN the worlds.

Alice and I remained friends after that first kiss. We kissed more times, though it never felt like that night, because how could it? We never dared call each other boyfriend or girlfriend. It seemed a test of fate, to use such words, such language, which might break what we had for so many years. The first time we went for drinks at Oly Pub, still not old enough for Indian laws but old enough for the languorously unperturbed servers in khaki, Alice kissed me right in front of her girl friends from school. They screamed and cheered like they were watching two of their favourite TV characters finally getting together, thumping the table till the beer bottles shook and the fried chicken liver quivered. The servers came by, finally perturbed, and asked us to please keep it down. Alice and her friends had just passed out of school days earlier. We drank till the world reeled, stomped down Park Street hand in hand and made out in a taxi while the driver glared at us in the rear view mirror. The next day, we crouched next to our landlines and told each other how much we threw up the previous night, how terrible was the fabled hangover, and how much we missed each other, though we were fifteen minutes apart. Then we did it all again, and again, if less recklessly. The bitter beer and acidic whiskey that tasted so awful to me at first soon went down easy, a Tea of Distraction if not Forgetfulness, a tincture that gave each night out with Alice the potential to last forever, pushing back the change that was coming.

Like her brother Francis, who had gone to culinary school in New York, Alice decided to apply to colleges in the United States. It felt inevitable. Some of her friends had already gone. Alice had only waited because she wanted to spend the year after school helping her parents out at the Crystal Dragon, and learning how to cook. That year slid out of reach slippery as an eel.

Alice told me on the night of her first show at the Princeton Club doing vocals for a local metal band called Raktagolla. Francis had been a guitarist for them before he left the city (he sold the guitar—Alice tried to learn, but never got the hang of it). I'd heard her sing before, but never with the band. In the cavernous magma-red dimness of the club, I went right up to the front of the dance floor and watched as Alice, cocooned in a kaleidoscope of stage lights, sang her heart out, her high notes riding the death growls, riffs and bashing drums of her bandmates, and I saw in her spotlit adulthood the years behind us, a younger Alice headbanging to her brother's Slipknot CD on the bed in between syrupy pop ballads. I couldn't tell how good Alice was, or how good the band was, because to me she was perfect.

Encore done, eardrums still vibrating from the noise, I clapped until my palms hurt. There were some whoops, and a decent smattering of applause from the half-full dance floor. Alice, shifting out of the siren confidence of her performance, looked embarrassed, but persevered and thanked her band members and the audience.

She told me about her college plans after the set, exchanging her coupons for rum and cokes for both of us at the bar. The drink was unwanted medicine in my throat, the nausea instant. I gulped it down like there was no alcohol in it. I told her I was proud of her decision, because I knew that's what a friend would do, should do.

"You can apply too. I know it's unlikely, but if we got into the same college, we could even go together," she said, a note of desperation in her voice—not necessarily to bring me with her, but to keep me from hurting with an illusion she already knew to be false. She looked obliviously, cruelly beautiful to me right then, in her dark lipstick and simple black tank top and jeans, hair down to her bare shoulders.

"I can't. I didn't even finish school," I looked at the ice melting in my lukewarm rum and coke.

"You would ace the essays. I'll help you and, you can study for the SATs. You're so smart, you can convince them if you just apply," she said.

I shook my head. She already knew. I could see it. "I can't, Tanu," I said, simply. I didn't go into how I didn't have a passport, how I doubted I could even get on a plane or cross borders, how I didn't really exist in the eyes of this gated world. I was, after all, a snake from nowhere.

"Don't worry about me," I said. "You're going to get in, and you're going to go to America and have an amazing time. You're going to blow them away like you did tonight's audience."

Over the thumping music, I didn't hear her sigh, but I saw her shoulders sag. "I was shit," she said half-heartedly, as if neither convinced of her talent or lack of. I slid my hand over the wet black marble of the bar, and placed it over hers. Her nails were short, painted in dark crimson polish. She accepted my touch, and smiled at me. That year, she got into a mid-tier liberal arts college in Pennsylvania with scholarship and aid. I expected she would—she had always been a good student. Her parents were happy to pay the remainder. Her father thought it was a waste to go all the way there and major in English literature like Alice was considering, but he was glad for the opportunities open to his daughter. Her mother, who had studied English at Jadavpur University in her youth, encouraged Alice wholeheartedly. Though Alice could barely eat for weeks in terror of not getting a student visa after the endless fees, tests, forms, and interviews, she did get one in the end. I can admit now I was secretly hoping she wouldn't, though I'd never have admitted it back then, even to myself.

~3~

THE WEEK BEFORE Alice left, I went over to the Tiretta Bazar flat to spend one last afternoon with her. She opened the door in pink pajama shorts and her familiar old Metallica T-shirt, now a better fit, its lettering cracked and faded like a tombstone. Her room was in a mess from packing. Her parents were out, her brother abroad, her grandparents in their flat upstairs. She was stormy with restrained anger, though she kept it from me with some effort, only snapping at times as I helped her pack. Sunlight from the verandah pranced around the room, contrary to the mood, thrown across the walls by the blades of the ceiling fan.

"No, don't fold those yet," she said. "I have a system. Just," she paced. "Sit down for a sec. Please." I sat on the bed. She sat on the chair next to her desk a few feet from me, littered with her old scrapbooks and yearbooks, pages filled with signatures and messages from her school friends.

"Are you okay?" I asked, obliviously.

She shook her head a little, not a full admission. "This was my last month here and you barely visited. You didn't have to wait until I called you."

"I...didn't want to get in the way of you spending time with your family. I thought you were busy preparing for everything."

She got up and paced. Framed in light from the verandah door, she looked at me.

"Ru, what are you going to do?"

"What do you mean?"

"You know what I mean. After I'm gone. If you can't go to college, then what?"

I felt a shame boiling inside me, oozing out as sweat. The room was hot, despite the fan. "Keep doing what I've always done. Living, I suppose."

She breathed out audibly, massaging her forehead. "You can't just sit in that house forever, doing nothing." She didn't quite finish saying *nothing*, stopping herself abruptly.

"I'm, happy for you. You know I am," I said. "But not everyone can go to college abroad like you."

"I know that. I didn't say college. I know you can't do that. Are you angry that I'm going to college? You can tell me if you are, I feel like you're holding something in, and it's not healthy."

"Why are you picking a fight right now?"

"I'm talking to you. I'm trying to talk to you and you keep refusing."

"Okay, fine. If you really want to do this now. Yes, I was upset when you told me. That you chose to go abroad instead of studying here, where you have friends."

"My school friends will be fine. You mean you. Where you are. Just say that," she said, and sat on the floor.

I didn't say anything, my heart racing.

"You can't expect me to be your one and only friend forever," said Alice. "That's not fair. You need to get out and do things. Without me. I can't be your entire life. I know it's tough because you're home-schooled, I just thought you'd have some kind of plan. Never mind."

I wanted her to stop. I didn't like feeling resentful towards her. "Maybe I'll write a book. Become a failed writer like my father."

"Your father's not a failed writer," she said, her tone softening. "He wrote a good book, didn't he? We read it. Parts of it. It was good."

"Well. Then I'll become a successful writer who isn't read by anyone, like my father."

"I'll read what you write. Promise you'll write it, and I'll read it," she said, tying socks into knots and shoving them into one of the open suitcases, pacing again. I didn't promise. She didn't seem to notice, moving back and forth between the piles of her belongings without any clear purpose.

"I wasn't upset at you," I said. "I was upset at the thought of you going away. I should have come to see you more often this month. You're right. But you know I'm proud of you, right? I really am. I want you to be happy."

She looked like she'd forgotten what she was doing, fidgeting rapidly with the hair tie on her wrist. "I know. Forget I said anything."

"Tanu—"

"I'm such a little shit," she said, slamming her strolly shut and surveying the clothes, underwear, books, CDs and plastic-wrapped personal hygiene products everywhere. "Making you help me pack." As I began to reassure her that I was happy to, she scrambled feline over the bed to me, and clamped her hand over my mouth. "Can I take off your clothes?" she asked, swallowing. I nodded, and she removed her hand, and then my clothes, her fingers shaking a bit and fumbling with my belt buckle, but ever so gentle as she pulled my jeans and boxers down. I helped her undress, unable to undo her bra, making her smile and take over. Naked, the afternoon reflections sluicing against us, we tasted each other with halting curiosity. She was salty from the August heat lingering on our flushed skin, pleasantly bitter around her neck where she'd put on a hint of perfume before I came over, despite her casual clothes. There was no song to mark the moment we saw each other without accoutrement, just the hum of the ceiling fan and the sound of late afternoon traffic downstairs. With no condoms at hand, Alice and I touched each other, lying on her bed amid the detritus of her unborn life abroad. She was wet, but I was soft. "It's okay," she said, stroking my hair, raking her nails soft against my scalp, her eyes shining. "My princess. My beautiful dragon queen." She kissed me deeply, slow and patient, until I grew hard in her hand, my fingers between her legs. Neither of us came before the doorbell rang and we scrambled to pull on our clothes, bodies feverish with unspent desire, limbs trembling, giggling and panicked, for a moment our impending farewell forgotten in a wash of endorphins and adrenaline. "Did you two fall asleep or what?" asked Auntie Chen at the door, unwisely, just about to use her keys.

AFTER ALICE'S PARENTS arrived, we did get some packing done. As sunlight faded from the room and the azaan lilted over the evening from the loudspeakers of mosques, I gave her the parting gift I'd stuffed deep in my jeans pocket, waiting for the right moment. It was a simple necklace—a polished black fang on a black cord.

"It's my grandmother's. I asked her. She liked the idea of you having it. It's not something that's been worn out, in the world. You should."

"It's gorgeous," Alice looked at the fang, rubbing the time-dulled tip that was once sharp enough to draw blood at the hint of a touch. Curved, it was the size of her bent pinky.

"It's a dragon tooth," I said. Alice looked up, startled. We hadn't talked too much about my family's 'culture' since the night we first kissed. "You can tell all your new friends in America any story you want. That it's from a tiger, or it's obsidian. Or tell them: it's from a young drake. The baby teeth of a growing serpent. My grandmother asked for it in exchange for a hundred drops of her own blood, a long, long time and place ago. There are more in the house, way bigger, earrings too, from claws and fangs. You saw some of them. But I know you prefer the smaller stuff. Now you can be a dragon queen too, whenever you want. If you want."

Alice held the necklace to her chest. "I. I'm not going to wear it now, okay? Because I don't want to explain what it is to my parents," her voice wavered, and she shook her head. "It's our secret. But I promise you I'm going to wear this on the plane, and pretend I'm riding on the back of a dragon when we're above the clouds. I'm going to wear it all the way there, and keep wearing it. I'm never going to never lose it. Thank you."

Auntie Chen shouted from the living room to come have tea. We did.

Soon after, Alice walked me downstairs. "I love you," she told me, under the streetlight that had stood sentinel by her verandah all the years of our sitting there. I told her I did too.

She didn't let me come with her parents to Dum Dum Airport the next week to see her off. I waited up late into the night for the Chens to call and say that she was safely through customs and in the air. So it was that the one true friend I had in all the world sailed to the other end of it in a metal beast that skirted the sky.

~1~

THEN THERE IS FIRST flight. How could I ever have forgotten it, without the aid of halahala, the dragon's tears, the gift of forgetfulness?

I think I was three or four years old. Once again, it was the courtyard of our house that was the cradle of impossibility, filled to the brim with moonlight and mist. This time I wasn't in my mother's arms, but strapped to her back with some strong, white fabric that shimmered as if woven from the dew that hung in the air. She was swathed in the same material, robes of it that hung loose over her body, and covered her hair and face. These clothes were covered head to toe in fine script, writing that crawled with each movement. Baba was similarly dressed, only his eyes visible, though he murmured lilting words to me in comfort. His feet, like Maa's, were tightly wrapped in the same material as their clothes, with no shoes. I had a thick woolen cap on my head, and was bundled in blankets. I don't know if I too wore the script-laced cloth that my parents wore on that night. As they moved, the material of their clothes almost disappeared, making me feel like I was hovering in the air instead of wrapped to the back of my mother. The garden shimmered in the voluptuous blue light, the plants and trees shifting restlessly. In the moonlight, the huge tree in the centre of the garden (whose eaves reached up beyond the roof) shifted with more than just a breeze, a gossamer glisten making it feel insubstantial, like a spider's web, like my parents' dresses. Within the net of its branches, something shifted that I'd never seen in that garden in all the years of playing in it day and night. Maa climbed the tree with me on her back, Baba following as my grandmother, grandaunts and granduncles sang softly down below. There were ropes leading up to the eaves, which they used for the climb, breathing heavy and even. As I looked up into the dizzy womb of branches, it felt like there was a kaleidoscope above me, as if the branches and leaves were breaking into pieces of light, not really there, that they were a skein hiding something that moved and hummed with the family's song.

And then, for a moment, I saw. That much of the tree's leaves and branches were an illusion painted on great wings that bristled and fluttered as we climbed. Reality slid liquid on the silken membranes of the beast that perched on top of the tall trunk and its naked branches. The bark, I saw as my mother traversed the trunk, was damp, breathing like it was alive. The tree wasn't quite a tree, and its crown certainly wasn't made up of leaves and branches. It was, in itself, an eyrie—a nest, cloaked in the great wings and breath of its occupant.

I don't know what my parents had fed me to keep me from terror, but I remember no fear, only a calm acceptance of what I was seeing. It felt like we were ascending into the night sky, and as we got closer to the crown of the tree, more of the heaving creature above us showed itself, coiled tight like a muscle under the skin of reality. My parents left the ropes, which were tied to the branches—or limbs, or tentacles—of its eyrie, and climbed over its form with practiced skill, toiling up the nonexistent branches and leaves that bristled all over it. Finally, they reached the top. To me, the family down in the courtyard felt kilometers below, their voices a whisper in the night as they sang on. My parents crouched low. They spoke to each other, to what was below us.

The top of the tree, its verdant moonlit eaves, slid like water off the back of the beast and its wings as they unfurled. I saw the span of its wings stretch dark across the top of the courtyard, from roof to roof. The vibrations of its rumbling body shook in my mother's body as well, in her bones and flesh. Baba moved close, hugging Maa from behind so I was sandwiched between them in their warmth. A blissful sense of peace came over me, like being wrapped in blankets in the dead of winter. I felt Baba's fingers at my lips, putting a wad of some kind of sugared dough in my mouth. *Babushona, chew this, don't swallow, your ears will feel funny but chewing will help*, he said. I understood enough to chew. I felt a pressure as he hugged me and Maa tight. My mother spoke louder in our fire tongue. I gazed at the iridescent slopes of the wings on either side of us, and the world tilted. I don't know how we stayed on our chariot, but we did. Bubbles of air burst in my ears, making my head ache. My gut jumped into my throat, and my weight fell out of me and into my father's body, leaving me weightless. The gum in my mouth was so sticky it glued to my teeth—otherwise I might have swallowed it by accident. From the misty stillness of the courtyard, we entered a storm of wind that roared in my ears through the woolen cap, a wintry explosion of icy air howling through the three of us. Even as I felt my parents shaking, the air changed and warmed, a heat from below sluicing the cold from the headwinds crashing into us. I saw moon and stars and sky through my squint, and I was afloat between my mother and father. There was no ground, only the wings stretched and sliding in and out of reality, steam rushing off their membranes which had turned the rich blue of night sky, stars sleeting down their planes. I floated as we ascended, our cutting speed turning the air into a hurricane, nothing but the roar in our ears and against our bodies, and everything tilted again.

Below us, below the huge living blades of the wings, was Calcutta like a smoky mirror reflecting the stars, streetlights and windows and cars drawing a luminous map across the Earth, which was blacker than the sky. High above us I saw another beast fly with us in the same direction, made of metal and light, growling into purpled clouds. The beast beneath us was silent except for its vibrations, which made everything hum, and the Earth below us shake in my eyes. I could hear only the sound of the passing air tearing as it hit the creature's wings, which barely moved, steam rushing off its crests so they were robed in streamers of cloud. The lights of Calcutta became smaller and smaller, until the moon drew a silver serpent along the waters of the Hooghly River, collared with the lights and metal of the Howrah Bridge. Clouds billowed by like ocean spray, cold and wet. My parents were shaking now, I realized, with laughter. Maa roared into the wind, knowing that her voice was so very small against the curve of an entire world.

And somehow, no one saw us. If they did, they saw a bat brushing against the moon. Because dragons aren't real. The city lights cascaded, fireflies in our wake. The stars were brighter, the moon reachable.

There we were, sky above and below us.

~2~

THE MEMORY OF my grandmother in the garden, tending the bush with her winged Bengal roses—that must have been our courtyard, unless there are other gardens with similar trees that we've visited, others of our people elsewhere in India. The bush grew, perhaps, into the great tree in the centre of our garden—the tree that was never actually a tree, but more an umbilicus and an eyrie. I have a vision of those Bengal roses maturing as the bush grew taller and they grew larger, their petalled wings drying and expanding in the sun as the tree drew on the energy of the earth, the world and its many dreams of dragons. The serpents eating their own tails when the time comes to close that circle, gnawing with the budding thorns of teeth through the stems that attached them to the branches of their world tree. The sap of their blood oozing down its branches and trunk, dampening the earth of the garden. Bats in the square of sky above the courtyard, fluttering through the gloaming every evening. Prey and companionship. I have a vision of the great tree burning as their tongues of fire grew long, the smoke and sparks rising into the sky alongside the spiraling heat of all the bonfires glimmering on the rooftops of wintry Calcutta, from all the Christmas and New Year's parties. My family singing, beating drums made from the membranes of wings. The tree shaking and writhing as its inhabitants clashed in loving battle with razored jaws and fire, fought to cull their numbers, realizing their own impossibility in this small, hard world with its polluted dreams. One of them painted in blood, growing the largest, feeding off the dreams of all the people in our house, in Bowbazar, in Calcutta, growing into a Queen atop the eyrie, robed in illusion.

How much halahala courses through my veins, churned by serpents in our garage? How much forgetfulness have I drunk at my parents' behest, to protect me from our impossibility?

~3~

IN THE GARDEN under the tree, I saw my grandmother fade into the air, as if I was looking at a reflection of her on a window pane. Her shadow flickered like her body couldn't catch the afternoon sunlight falling on it. I walked up to her in halting steps, almost expecting to slam into a glass pane out of nowhere, and touched her shoulder, startling her. To my relief, she was as solid as she ever was. I could see the grass flattening under her chappals, the faint veins of talcum in the creases of her skin, the silvered cords of her pleated hair falling like ropes down her back, the inky black of her wonderfully dark eyes as she looked at me. She looked surprised, eyes glazed.

"Babu, oh," she said. "I thought you were…your grandfather. You look so much like them."

"Didima, are you feeling unwell?"

"I…thought I was gone, there, for a second. You saw it, didn't you?"

"I didn't. I don't. I don't know."

"You did. I'm fading. Like your grandfather did. It's why I thought of them when I saw your face."

"You're fine. You're healthy and fine."

"Uff, my knees disagree. Come," she said, walking with me to the verandahs around the courtyard and sitting with a grunt on one of the chairs facing the garden. There was a sudden pall over the courtyard, the sunlight turned to cloudy light. I sat on the chair next to hers.

"I'm very old, babu. Don't look so worried. It is inevitable."

"You're not fading away. There's no such thing. I refuse to believe that."

Didima smiled, smoothing her robes, which had shimmered and changed from white to glittery, inky blue in the change of light. "Belief is a serpent eating its tail forever, knowing that its tail is finite." She closed her eyes and gripped the arms of the wooden chair. "Oh. No avoiding it. Existing can be a pain, na?" she laughed.

"Ei, don't be so sad," she said, taking a deep breath and looking at me. "Tell me something nice, quick. Tell me how your friend is, the one who went abroad. Tanu. How is she?"

"We should be talking about what's happening—"

"It's simple. I'm fading. Talking helps keep me here. So talk."

I shook my head, wiping my eyes and holding her hand. She squeezed mine. "Alice is fine. Doing well," I said.

"You never talk about her anymore. Did she find a boyfriend over there or what?"

I smiled, though I scarcely felt like I could at that moment. "She did, but they broke up. She has a girlfriend now. She met her in the metal band they play in, in college."

"Oh. There you are."

"She hasn't told her family. Doesn't know when she will, if she will. So you stay mum, Didima."

"Psht. You know me, the neighborhood gossip. I barely even understand what's going on beyond the walls of this house nowadays. Like what is a metal band?"

"It's a group that plays a kind of loud music. We told you about it before. I don't like it that much, but she and her brother were always into it. The band is pretty good. Alice was always a great singer."

"Mm. You two were so close. Is that why you never mention her now? Her metal musical girlfriend?"

"I'm glad for her. There's nothing to mention. She's living her life."

"Mmm, good. It's good. Young people being the way they want, whether or not the world wants it." She looked at me. "You miss her a lot. I can tell."

I didn't deny this, nor say anything.

"But take solace. She's still here, in this world, and so are you. Does she still write to you?"

"Sometimes, we do. Email. She sends me digital photos. Lots of pictures of her cooking for her friends at their dorm. She looks happy." Alice had made me an email account before she left. Though we no longer wrote to each other often, I checked it at cyber cafes every week, just in case.

"I don't understand all this digital, email, cyber. But if it helps you stay in touch, do that. She's a sweet girl. Is she wearing the necklace you gave her?"

"She loved it, Didima. I'm sure she is."

"Good, good. That necklace hadn't been in the sky for a long time."

"You flew here, like she flew to America. Didn't you."

She looked thoughtful, drowsy as she looked out to the garden, at the tree that rose up out of our vision. "Yes, we flew."

"Before there were planes," I said.

She chuckled. "No need to remind me how old I am. But yes, before." She looked at me, her face serious. "You should stop drinking the halahala. Enough is enough."

"Why?"

"You know why. It's not really working anymore. It does you no good."

"Maa and Baba won't—"

"Tch. They're giving it to you out of habit. They know there's no point anymore, they won't say anything." Didima sighed. "I was always against it. But...don't be too angry at your parents, babu. They've made mistakes, I know, and so have I. Your parents were very scared when they had you. Right out there, under that tree," she pointed at the garden. There was a breeze rustling the grass despite the garden being walled in by the house, the eaves of the tree filling the courtyard with its susurrus.

"You came out of your mother and into my hands, drawn by this world's gravity, ground below you. Your body chose this place. You were conceived here. Not like us. Your Maa-Baba wanted to respect that. To make this reality safe for you. Even if they didn't know what they were doing."

"Wait. You're saying my parents weren't born here either?"

Didima put her hands on her wide belly. "I carried your mother across realities inside me. She was born on the long trip here, both of us on the back of the serpent. Your Baba... he was little, where we came from. He lost his parents young. The clan took care of him and raised him together. His mother was killed during the violence when we left. She was a great warrior, a very skilled dragoner. We lost his father here—some just didn't have the will, to live in this world." My grandmother paused. "My beloved also. They missed home too much and, well. Faded. Your parents grew up in this world, but they are not of it. They were already together in affection, and proud young people of the clan by the time we came to this city, and raised this house to be a dragons' nest."

"When the house was built? That means…"

"They're a lot older than they look, yes. We all are, except for you. Our people are one with the serpent impossible. It teaches you to swim different through space and time. We too are impossible, like the serpent, or halfway so. We forget that, here."

"You said my grandfathers, they missed home and faded. Do you miss home too? Is that why," I said, my throat heavy.

The garden stuttered as lightning speared the clouds somewhere high above. There was no rain. Didima spoke in the fire tongue. "Let me tell you something about the dragoner clans of Calcutta. When we settled here, our people went childless. That was our way. We are long lived, after all, and to raise children in between worlds while hiding in plain sight of a reality that didn't want us, was seen as beckoning ill fate. This was a communal sacrifice to the serpent—our dreams of a new generation here given way, so that the dream of one day returning to our homeworld may be kept alive.

"You were not expected. Some were displeased by your parents' decision. Some saw it as a new promise. Some stopped visiting the Dragoners Club, seeing this house as bad luck. Some who lived here left to make their own way. Others kept the club alive, and our lives went on. I don't know of any other child born to this community, in this city, but who can say. But time flows different here. It caught up to us, and our long lives began to flicker out. I don't know how other clans have fared across the city, or this nation, or this world. But everyone who lived in this house eventually faded from this reality. I know you have some memory of them, your uncles and aunties. But your parents and I lasted longer after them all. We had you to take care of. Make of that what you will.

"So yes, I do miss the home where I was born, on the distant shores of another reality. But it's this world in which I saw my grandchild grow up into a beautiful person. For that alone I am grateful to be on Earth. I've already lived far longer than this world allows. You're here to remember me. That's all that matters."

I said nothing, because there was nothing to be said. I couldn't speak. Leaves danced in the air of the courtyard on a cool wind. It blew them into the verandah, rustling against the stone floor. Thunder, somewhere far.

Didima raised her hand to my face, stroking my cheek.

"My babu. So gentle. You'll feel things with all your heart. It will keep you on Earth."

I REMEMBER EVERYTHING now, because my family is gone.

The house is empty. The Bowbazar Dragoners Club is shut, nothing but dust and light on its tables. The aquariums in the garage are empty, corners clotted with moss. The Crystal Dragon Restaurant Cum Bar lives on, but it has always been barricaded from the fickle nature of the nest around it. Nonetheless, it is closed and quiet now, soon to be renovated under the stewardship of Francis Chen.

Baba wrote, so I do too. So many years of learning in this house, eating my own tail. A student of the world, but not a part of it. I feel like I am inside an egg, waiting for someone to tap the shell.

~4~

A MEMORY: MY parents, wrapped in their riding dress, shimmering in and out of reality under another winter sky. Maa hugged me, like she never does. She was crying, like she never does, like she didn't even when her mother ceased to exist a year earlier. Baba hugged me too, and I was caught between the two of them, between two memories.

"Can you ever forgive us?" Maa asked me, her face crawling with tattoos. The ink looked fresh because of her tears. My father looked away. He couldn't look me in the eye.

I don't know if I truly did, or truly could. "There's nothing to forgive, Maa. You did what you thought was right, to protect me," I said.

Maa's face crumpled, and I felt as if my heart had stopped existing, like them. "My baby," she said, swallowing the sob that nearly surfaced, her jaw clenched like the mother of old. "It's becoming impossible…"

"To exist," I said, nodding. They'd been fading for months now, without the help of dragon silk scarves or riding clothes, their bodies sometimes sieving light, reflections of themselves on a pane of glass. "I understand. I understand who my people are. I understand why you hid that from me," I said.

"If there were any other way, we would take it," said Maa. "A Queen needs the clan, we are one body. Now that everyone's gone, especially after your grandmother, it is struggling. It can't lend us its power, to stay real here, any longer. It yearns for home, and calls out in our dreams. Whether or not we can find our way back, or if it's safe there, we must try, or fade like everyone else."

"Please," said Baba. He faced me, though his eyes still couldn't meet mine. "Come with us."

"You know I can't. I'm too much a part of this world."

Maa placed a hand on my chest. "If we knew this was how it would be, we would have done things differently. We thought we could give you a life here, in this crowded world, keep you from the impossibility of who we are. But you kept remembering."

She clutched my sweater. Her face set into that familiar, stoic expression. "There is nothing I will regret more in this life, or any other. We thought we were protecting you from... this. From fading away."

Baba shook his head. "Let's just take him, see what—"

"To ride upon a Queen through the slipstream of realities could kill him with no experience. If we had let the bond form... It protects us, it may not protect him. Don't ask me to risk that. Don't ask him. The serpent is weak from the loss of our clan, from the polluted dreams of this world tearing itself apart. We might not even find our way back home."

"Don't say that," I held Maa's hand, which was icy. "If you can't find your way home, you will find a place, like Earth once was, where the serpent impossible can fly free on sky and land, where the world trees can grow higher than the roof of a house, and stretch into the clouds again. Where you can be dragoners again. But you will find home. I know it. It wants to go back, even I can feel that. It will find a way."

"He always remembered more than we ever thought," said Baba, trying to smile.

My mother closed her eyes, shaking her head. "No. No. No. Your father's right. This isn't right. What if we're making another huge mistake, like the one we made, not teaching you? Just come with us. If we can…"

"Maa," I said. She fell silent. "I trust you. It's difficult, after all these years. But I do. You and Baba are dragoners, you always have been. I can tell, I can tell you know that I wouldn't survive. Not like this. So go in peace. I trust you. I trust you to find our home."

She gripped my shoulder hard. "Don't let go of the house. It is a dragons' nest, its structure will hold for a long time yet. Do not question its existence, do not try and sell it, or make it more of this world, or its illusion may collapse entirely. Everything in the life we built is connected to this place. The money we get from the Chens, from savings, that we use and pretend has value like the rest of the people on this planet believe. It is linked to this nest that the dragons wove. You must keep faith, or the scrying eyes of this world's empires will realize that the Chens are essentially paying no one that is written into their books and accounts of who is real."

"I'll try, Maa."

"This place is your birthright. It will be difficult for you, the way we've left you in between worlds. But this is your home, and it will keep you safe. With any luck, there is more life left in it than we think. Heed what grows here, and pay attention. Let it remain true. Do you understand?"

"I'll take care of it. I promise."

My father was trembling with silent pain. I couldn't bear to see it, and pulled him closer by the arm. "I'll write a book, Baba. Like you. To remember you both, to remember our people." He nodded, breathless, and managed a smile this time. "Babu, we'll come back for you if we can. We're more like you than you know. The serpent carries the memory of our clan, and we carry that knowledge, as part of it. But we have no memories of our own, of home. We don't know what we'll find there, whether we'll be welcome there. Maybe one day…maybe we can come back, if the serpent wills it."

"Or maybe I can find my way there."

"All of this is impossible. Why not one more thing," said Maa, soft. "Our separation will be a sacrifice, to keep a dream of our reunion alive." My mother looked at the world tree above us, so tall yet stunted, kept from reaching beyond the roof of the sky. "You were born right here," she said.

"Under the wings of a serpent impossible," I said.

The crown of the world tree curled and writhed, reality warping as wings shivered. The serpent flexed its miraged skin, tail coiling in an eternal spiral down the trunk of its eyrie. Four fractal flowers of starlight danced above us among the branches, and a jagged wound appeared in reality, a maw opening. It was the first time I looked into the Queen's eyes. I couldn't help my tears. Maa's hands tightened around mine. Baba stepped forward and kissed my cheek, his now whitening beard brushing against me.

"We're sorry, Ru," said my mother. In the fire tongue, she spoke my name as given under the serpent that watched my birth. "Exist, like we never allowed you." With that, she covered her face with her riding mask. So did my father. They waved in silent farewell.

THE SQUARE OF sky above the courtyard, eclipsed by vast wings that cut through reality, a tail tracing a bristling map across the stars in a curving lash. Then there was nothing but the bare tree in the courtyard, shorn of leaves, suddenly smaller and shorter. There was a rumble of thunder, though there were only a few clouds smeared across the moon. The searing trail of a shooting star blazed across the night, but it went from horizon to void, a light leaving the world.

I walked inside my empty house, and looked at the last cup of the Tea of Forgetfulness, which my parents brewed for me. They left many bottles of it. It's weak, diluted, useless. It is for the pain. I don't drink it.

THIS IS NOT A book like the one Baba wrote. But it is a beginning.

I write it for my family. I write it for my people. There are more of the clans out there—or if there aren't, it is a dream I must keep alive. I write it for you—the others I will meet as a human being on this forsaken world, who know nothing of true impossibility. Now that my people are gone, with their mastery of illusion, will this entire house disappear if I leave it and enter the rest of the world? How flimsy is this story they've woven around me, their child of Earth? I will find out, eventually. I promised my mother, and my father, and my grandmother. I must have faith.

"I'M SORRY I made you visit so early. It's the best time for what I want to show you," I tell Alice, leading her into the house she hasn't been inside for years, but spent so much time inside, an age ago.

"That's okay," she laughs. "Jet lag had me up at dawn anyway. I actually like the walk here so early. Nice and empty, just the doggies and shopkeepers. Don't I get a hug after so long?" We hug, polite, brief. She looks tired, from flying across the world a day ago, from saying goodbye to her friends and lovers and the place she called home for four years. She plans to apply to graduate programs abroad for a master's in English Literature, but she is here for now, to help her family with the restaurant once more. We have met a few times over the years during her rare visits home, usually among her school friends. I've seen glimpses of the changes that merge with my memories of her—the little tattoo of a winged serpent on the inside of her left wrist, the sheen of blue in her bob cut. She's wearing her old Slipknot T-shirt under a loose unbuttoned cardigan. On the shirt's faded lettering, over her chest, lies a single black fang, the old black thread that was strung through it replaced with a thin metal chain. She sees me looking at it.

"Didn't lose it," she says.

"Thank you. For taking care of it. I wish Didima could see you wearing it."

"Me too," she says. She had written me a long email when I'd told her my grandmother died, and offered to call. I told her not to. She follows me as I take her to the courtyard.

"So...are you okay?" she asks, hesitantly. "You sounded, weird, on the phone."

"I'm. I just want to show you something I found in the house. Something has happened that...I didn't think would happen. I really think you would like to see it. I hope I'm right," I tell her. We walk out on to the grass of the garden, pale and dry from fresh winter. In the morning, by the golden light that pours into our empty chasm of the courtyard, I stand under the withered world tree. "God, the house looks so huge now, without anyone here," says Alice, looking around, her voice echoing across the looming walls and concentric verandahs rising to the sky. "How are your parents doing in Assam, by the way?"

"Tanu," I say, stepping back towards the trunk of the tree. I pinch nothing in front of me, run my fingers down from my neck to my feet, and turn the air inside out. My jeans and T-shirt ripple into nothingness to reveal the dragon silk robe I am wearing, one which belonged to my mother. The fire tongue on its fabric crawls in living shimmer across my body, commanded to stay its illusion.

"What the...fuck," says Alice, eyes wide. I part the invisible headscarf I'm wearing, and let my hair fall. What looked like shoulder-length hair cascades down my back and shoulders, to my waist. A curved dragon's tooth hangs from my ear, stretching the lobe with its weight, anchored to me through a hole my mother pierced before she left.

"It's not a magic trick," I tell Alice softly. "It's a traditional dress." I speak the word for it in the fire tongue. "My mother taught me to wear it before she left. It can rewrite what people see over it, if understood and worn correctly. She taught me every word that shines on its fabric. My parents didn't move to Assam, Alice. They had to leave the world. To find home again, out there."

I can see the recognition in Alice's face, years of forgetting what brush she had with the impossible in this house, evaporating in the shock of seeing it clear as a winter morning on my body. "Oh, fuck," she says, softly. Her eyes dart wildly against the script glistening and moving against the fabric, the way the folds almost vanish, letting light pass through me, slivers of invisibility that run up and down the shape of my existence. "My god. These clothes are in your father's book. It's…real. I can't believe it."

"You can. I saw that you wanted to, all those years ago." I hold out my open hand. She doesn't take it.

"Your parents—they left? You're all alone?"

"I'm too much of Earth. They couldn't take me. But we made what peace we could. I'm here to remember them. They taught me more before they left than in my whole life. Like my name." I tell Alice the true name given to me under the serpent impossible in a tongue from another reality.

Alice steps back, shaking her head. "Are you," she swallows. "Is this real?" she asks, with heartbreaking sincerity.

I kneel down before her and lower my head, letting my tresses touch the grassy ground. "Alice, you are my friend. You are the only person on Earth, not of my clan, who has truly known me. I swear to you by the serpent impossible, by the ocean above, by the honour of my clan, that there is no deceit or malice here. You are safe here, I promise you." I keep my head lowered, the silence filled by the sound of crows cawing on the verandah rails.

I do not raise my head. I hear the sound of her sneakers against the soil. Her fingers against my hair. "Ru. Get up, please." I do, her hands moving to my face, and down my hair. "I'm sorry—your name," she says.

"Ru's still fine too," I say.

"I want to say your other name. I just, might need some practice."

"I'll teach you, if you want. There is time."

She looks at me, her face pale. "This looks beautiful on you. You look like...you. You look so lovely," she says, her voice breaking.

"So do you," I say, and she laughs.

"I'm dressed like I just rolled out of bed. I might as well be still in bed. Stupid to say I feel like I'm dreaming, like a character in a movie, but. I can't..."

She stops herself saying *believe*.

"I have so much to show you," I tell her. "If you want to see it. The choice is yours entirely. Your life in this reality will change forever, if you choose to see, to believe. If it's too much, I understand. Just ask, and there's a way to forget.

All you have to do is drink a cup of disgusting tea, and I'll change out of these clothes, and we'll go have early morning Chinese breakfast at Tiretta Bazar and it'll be like nothing happened. Okay?"

She nods, looking terrified, calm, no longer tired.

"We have to climb the tree."

Under the eaves, I touch the air between us, pluck it. A cord of light shivers, resolves iridescent into a silken rope that hovers on the edge of reality like my clothes. "Hold to this, it won't break. Nor will the branches of the tree. It'll be easier if you go barefoot." Alice leaves her sneakers and socks on the grass, and follows me up the trunk, gripping the rope, taut and sticky in our hands. Our toes curl into the bark, which is both slippery and covered in fine fur which clings to our skin, giving us purchase as we clamber up. I can hear her heavy breaths behind me. Together we climb into the dew-slick branches, a fractal universe of ever-breaking sunlight all around us. I help Alice up into the cradle of the tree, spangled with the warmth of the growing morning light. Her cheeks, fuller from the years of American food, are red, her face damp. "Ohf, god, this is too much exercise this early," she huffs as I take her arm. For a moment, all impossibility is gone, and we may as well be children playing, though we never climbed the tree when we were teenagers. The dragon tooth dangles from her neck. She curls up next to me, our hips and arms touching. As she recovers her breath, her bare feet perched against bark next to mine, impossibility returns, and she falls silent. In the world of the tree's crown